BUCHANAN'S MANHUNT

Buchanan had been on the frontier since he was fourteen and bore the scars of a hundred battles. But in his heart, Buchanan was a peaceable man. It's just that trouble and danger seemed to stalk him. An escaped convict had shot down a friend. Now Buchanan had to track him down—and the innocent young girl he had taken hostage.

Books by Jonas Ward
in the Linford Western Library:

BUCHANAN SAYS NO
BUCHANAN ON THE PROD
BUCHANAN'S RANGE WAR
BUCHANAN'S STAGE LINE
BUCHANAN'S GAMBLE
TRAP FOR BUCHANAN
BUCHANAN'S MANHUNT

JONAS WARD

BUCHANAN'S MANHUNT

Complete and Unabridged

LINFORD
Leicester

First Linford Edition
published September 1989

British Library CIP Data

Ward, Jonas
 Buchanan's manhunt.—Large print ed.—
 Linford western library
 I. Title
 813'.54[F]

 ISBN 0-7089-6760-4

Published by
F. A. Thorpe (Publishing) Ltd.
Anstey, Leicestershire
Set by Rowland Phototypesetting Ltd.
Bury St. Edmunds, Suffolk
Printed and bound in Great Britain by
T. J. Press (Padstow) Ltd., Padstow, Cornwall

1

THE sun beat down on the desert, scorching the Stetson perched on Buchanan's sandy head. There was a squared circle of loose ropes, the posts driven into the earth only that morning. In the ring was Coco Bean. Facing him was the giant Yaqui known as El Diablo. Both fighters were bare-fisted and exuding quarts of salty perspiration.

The horses were lined nearby, toward the border. They were only fifteen miles from Yuma, but the desert lay in between. Buchanan did not like the setup.

The captain of the *rurales* held the stake —only two thousand, but all they could afford. The Mexicans had demanded that Coco fight their champion. Two thousand wasn't enough to risk what Buchanan was afraid they were risking.

All else being equal, they could win and lose the stake if the burly, mustachioed captain refused to hand over the money. There were enough natives, Indians and *rurales* to make it stick. But this was not the worst Buchanan expected.

On the other hand, there was Sheriff Jake Lee of Yuma, a stubborn, brave man. There was Amsy Burke, old friend to Buchanan, the one-armed guard of Yuma Territorial Prison on leave of absence. There was Burke's friend, the smallish, innocent-looking Cole Conrad. If these professed allies stood firm, Buchanan argued with himself, something might be accomplished.

Coco Bean was doing his part. The black champion was walking around the huge Indian, taking his time, picking his shots. He had already hit the Yaqui with everything but the ring posts. He was saving the big punch for the time when Buchanan had figured out a play and could give the signal. Coco stuck a left fist to El Diablo's nose and brought blood. There was a dangerous silence.

The Mexicans had insisted that the Americans come unarmed, El Diablo's people had been all smiles and full of promises and blandishments. This alone had been reason for Buchanan to wear the big belt buckle which concealed the little Derringer that was so deadly at close quarters. Amsy, also forewarned, had a revolver concealed beneath the stump of his left arm. Sheriff Lee had a six-gun under his saddle blanket. Only Conrad seemed to be without a weapon.

Buchanan said, "I don't like it no way."

He was six feet four inches tall and almost half as wide. He had sandy hair and greenish eyes. He bore the scars of a hundred battles. He had been on the frontier since fourteen, when he had gone up the trail to Abilene. He was from East Texas, but his adopted home was the high country of New Mexico.

In his heart he was a peaceable man. He detested this sort of situation and felt a bit of a fool for allowing it to take place. Coco had needed the money, and bets had been made, and Buchanan had given in against his better judgment. He looked over at his big horse, Nightshade, and saw that the sensitive creature was pawing the ground, restless, smelling danger.

Sheriff Lee said, "If they pull anything on us, I'll forget the law and bring a bunch down here."

"And they'll be long gone," Buchanan said. "No, we got to figure to get away without the money."

"That *rurale* mustache is holdin' the bets, too," said Amsy Burke.

"Some of it my money," the sheriff added. "The hell with lettin' 'em get away with anything, Buchanan."

Burke turned to the mild-appearing Conrad. "You got any ideas, Cole?"

"Well, maybe a little bitsy one."

"Then go do it," said Burke. Conrad drifted away, and the prison guard said to Buchanan, "He's a smart little jasper. Knows more tricks 'n a monkey on a stick."

"Monkeys don't count," said Buchanan. "What we need here is some fire power."

Coco, sweating like a bull, moved around the big Indian and looked appealingly at his corner. Buchanan shook his head. Coco continued to spar.

"If there was a chance of makin' a run across the desert," Buchanan said to the sheriff, "if you think we can hold 'em off and make it, I'd give a try. Forget the money. I got a feelin' we ain't goin' to get it."

"Can Coco knock that big Injun out?"

"Any time I give him the word."

Cole Conrad came drifting back. He said, "You're right, Buchanan. I smell it. The captain, he no talk straight. You know what I mean?"

"I know."

"I'd tell your guy to win and make a run for it," said Conrad. "I'll grab his clothes and take them along. Amsy can cut the picket line and use that gun of his'n for a small stand-off. Sheriff, you game for it?"

"I want that bettin' money." Jake Lee had a stubborn streak, of which Buchanan was well aware.

"Forget it," said Burke. "Buchanan and

5

Cole, they got the way to go. The only way."

Buchanan made his decision. He took off his hat and wiped his brow with his bandanna. In the ring, Coco showed white teeth in a grateful grin. He walked inside a left lead and hit El Diablo in the belly with a tremendous right hand. He stepped back.

The Yaqui doubled over. Coco measured him. He hit him on the jaw. El Diablo spun around. Coco, saving his hand, struck again for the body. El Diablo went down and lay quivering in the dry dust.

The captain of *rurales* howled. The referee, a tall, thin Mexican, lifted a hand and yelled, "Foul! I give the fight to El—"

He never finished the sentence. Buchanan, already in the ring to warn Coco, swung a fist. The referee went flying from the force of the punch, to the ropes, over the top of the rope, into the advancing captain, clearing out two of the armed *rurales*. Bedlam ensued.

The little group, with Coco still clad in

long johns and soft shoes and nothing else, ran for their horses. Their guns came into view. Buchanan mounted Nightshade and led the way to the edge of the Yuma Desert. They were gone before a shot could be fired after them.

It was a hot journey, but the horses were rested, and they had been watered. Buchanan wondered if they could all make it under the circumstances. If the ride had been longer, he knew they could not.

He slowed down, looking back. They were coming, on wiry Indian ponies that were desert-wise. They were riding like fiends, some were already loosing rifle shots into the air.

Buchanan asked, "Now why in thunder are they so riled? They got the money. The crook that was referee give the fight to their man."

He looked to one side, and Cole Conrad was spurring his horse. He saw fear in the small man then. *Not the man to stick in a tight spot*, he thought. On his other side, Amsy Burke rode up, grinning.

Burke said, "Forgot to tell you, Tom. Cole's a tricky little devil. Got the fastest hands in the West."

"Uh-huh. Fast hands."

"He's, uh, real good at cards and all. And—uh—pickin' pockets."

Buchanan said, "He got the stakes?"

"He got 'em. He's goin' to split back with us. He knows I'm onto him. He picked 'em from El Capitán, there."

Buchanan said, "Nightshade, carry us onward."

The black horse responded, but the other mounts were not so strong. Buchanan held back, feeling helpless but unwilling to desert his companions. Coco was a heavyweight; fortunately he was riding a sturdy cob from the livery stable. Conrad was lightweight and seemed able to stick to his chestnut. Amsy Burke had been a wrangler in his youth, and rode a gray which had bottom. They plugged along. The pursuit gained every step of the way, but the way, Buchanan reckoned, was short.

Sheriff Lee pulled up alongside

8

Buchanan as Burke fell back, producing his revolver. "What's that I heared? Conrad pinched the poke?"

"Uh-huh," said Buchanan. "How's that nag of yours?"

"Strong."

Buchanan said, "Amsy, pass me that gun you hid."

Burke hesitated, scowling. "Now, Tom, don't do one of them loco things of yourn."

Buchanan took the extended revolver. He looked at Lee, who had his own gun raised and ready. "A little *pasear?*"

"Sure enough." Lee had always been braver than he was smart. He wheeled his fleet roan. Buchanan kneed Nightshade into a parabola. They headed back toward the motley pursuers.

Before the Mexicans were in range, the sheriff and Buchanan began firing. Elevating the sights, they dropped bullets just ahead of the angry crew.

Taken completely by surprise, the Mexican *rurales* and the Indian scattered. Some of them turned back.

9

Burke, Coco, and Conrad had gained a half-mile by the time the enemy found themselves and returned the fire. Bullets sang their little bee song around the heads of Buchanan and Lee, who swung their horses around and put on speed. They flew through the blinding heat, sand scattering beneath their hooves.

Buchanan shouted, "Just keep goin', Jake. Don't try to reload. There ain't any time."

"Don't you worry none," panted the sheriff. "Just keep pluggin' along. I think we saved us five minutes."

"Uh-huh," said Buchanan. "Just pray it's enough."

"You reckon they'll cross the border after us?"

Buchanan grinned at him. "Nope."

"Why not? We got their money."

Buchanan said, "Called a friend of mine."

"Oh," said the sheriff. "I see."

They covered their mouths with their kerchiefs against the swirling sand. They rode.

Behind them came the angry horde. Three or four gained by leaps and bounds on their ponies. Buchanan glanced back again, then drove Nightshade onward.

The border was plainly marked. They charged across, with leaden bullets now flying closer and closer. The pursuit would gladly break international law in the name of greed and vengeance, Buchanan knew. He gave a loud halloo.

Men came riding from a clump of yucca. They bore long guns and wore range clothing and a certain kind of Stetson and on their vests were badges. They lined up in semi-military fashion as Buchanan rode up to them.

The leader said, "How'd it go, Tom?"

"Not real good," Buchanan told them. "It was a frameup. But we got the money. See you in the Yuma Palace."

The pursuers were reining in. They had experience with this group. The border patrols were Arizona Rangers, second only in reputation to the better known Texas outfit. They did not fire a shot. They merely sat on their horses with rifles at the ready.

The mob from below the border pulled around. They debated. Buchanan waited. Then the captain of *rurales* shook a fist and led his followers back the way they had come. Buchanan wondered fleetingly how the real victim, El Diablo, was feeling at this moment.

The streets of Yuma had been made wide to accommodate twenty-mule teams; that allowed so much more dry dust to kick up beneath the heels of Buchanan's handmade boots. He said to the stable boy, "Walk this horse dry, then feed him slow and careful. This weather is hard on horseflesh."

"Man flesh too," said the boy. He accepted a silver dollar, his eyes brightening. "This'll go to gettin' me the hell out of here and over into California."

Nobody wanted to remain in Yuma, Buchanan thought, making his way to the saloon misnamed the Palace. The others were already there, not so concerned about their nags. They sat around a poker table, waiting. Buchanan waved to the bartender to bring cold beer and sat down, swishing the dust from his hat, sighing.

Amsy Burke said, "They tell a story about one of the prisoners. He died and went to hell. Two days later he sent back for his blankets."

"I believe it," said Buchanan. He looked at Sheriff Jake Lee. "What you doin' in a hellhole like this?"

"Gettin' ready to quit and leave."

"Conrad?"

"Just passin' through," said the small man. He produced a flat packet. "Everybody speak up, and I'll count out his share of the loot."

Amsy Burke said, "Hand it over, Cole. I seen you deal. I'll count it out."

Conrad smiled without rancor. "You think I'd try to fool around with this crowd? I ain't loco."

Coco stretched long arms above his head. "We done had trouble enough for one day. Time to unlax. Take it easy. Money ain't everything."

13

"Sure beats what comes second, though," said Conrad.

Burke was dealing out the money, the stakes to the bettors, two thousand to Coco. He said, "My last night to take it easy. I got to go back to that hellhole tomorrow. Y'know, I feel plumb sorry for some of those people in the jail."

"They belong there," the sheriff reminded him.

"I know, I know. But that's a terrific bad place to be cooped up. Too many of them die on us."

"It's the law," Lee insisted.

"I know it. But I don't have to like it." He lifted his stump of an arm. "Ain't many jobs open for me."

They drank beer, not cold but better than nothing. Buchanan wiped his brow. Coco looked at him.

"We goin' to get out of here tomorrow for sure. I'll buy me a horse. Okay?"

"Uh-huh," said Buchanan. He turned to Amsy. "I'll look around the high country. Maybe I can find something for you."

Burke said, "Not much chance." He

14

grinned. He lifted his glass. "I got another problem you know about damn well. I like my booze too much."

"You can work on that if you want."

Burke grew serious. "Man with one arm out here ain't worth a hell of a lot no way. Lee, here, he's been good to me."

The phlegmatic lawman moved uneasily. "I know you got a tough bunch in there. I know how it is to handle 'em."

Burke said, "I'm the easy mark. Even Rube Farnum says I'm easy."

Buchanan asked in surprise, "You got Farnum in there?"

"You know Rube?"

"Some time ago," said Buchanan. "He was a hiyu sorta *hombre* when I knew him. Smart and tough."

"Got to robbin' banks, he was so clever," said Burke. "Then he kilt a cashier and didn't quite get away. That was in Tucson."

"How long has he been in?"

Burke considered. "Reckon it's about five years."

"Five and a half," said Conrad.

Everyone stared at the small man who had hitherto been silent. He shrugged, smiling in his easy manner.

"Case made a big splash in the papers. I was in California. Heard a lot about Farnum there, too."

"Wasn't he from California?" asked Buchanan.

"I believe so," said Conrad. He fell silent again, playing with a deck of cards, fanning them, manipulating them in his surprisingly large, supple hands.

Burke said, "Whyn't you come out and take a look-see at the jail afore you leave, Tom? Cole's comin' out tomorrow mornin', seein' his train's not 'til noon."

"Train? By golly, I'd forgotten the Southern and Pacific came through here in '78. Come in from over in California, didn't it?"

"That's right. You ain't been here for a long time," said Sheriff Lee. "Rails is all that kept Yuma goin'. I come with the rails, so to speak."

The captain of the Arizona Rangers entered the saloon. Buchanan waved him over. He accepted a beer, then said, "Sure wish I could rally around tonight. But we got notice there's some Apache trouble up north. No rest for the wicked, they say. No rest for nobody, I say."

"Sure do thank you," Buchanan said.

"We saw that run you and Jake made. That was sweet."

"Old story." Buchanan laughed. "People chasin' someone reminds me of cats and dogs. You ever notice? Dog'll chase a cat 'til the cat's cornered. Cat turns and shows how it is. Dog backs off."

"Seen it with all kinds of animals." The Ranger finished his beer, waved a hand and was gone.

Cole Conrad asked, "So that was why you two done it?"

"Buyin' a little time," said Buchanan.

"You could easy have got kilt."

"You figure which way the odds are best," Buchanan said. "You ought to know about odds."

"Me?" Conrad looked surprised.

"You're somethin' of a gambler, ain't you?"

17

Conrad laughed softly. "Not if people know me. Or if there's anybody around might know about me."

Burke added, "Nobody with good sense would play against him, Tom. Deal a hand for him, Cole."

The small man offered the cards for a cut. Buchanan obliged. The pasteboards riffled around, floating to drop precisely in front of each man.

"Turn 'em over," suggested Amsy.

Coco had a straight. Buchanan had a full house. The sheriff had three tens. Amsy had a flush. Cole showed his. He had four aces.

"Ain't but one man I ever saw do that," said Buchanan.

"Luke Short," acknowledged Conrad. "I tried cheatin' him one time."

"He saw you cut the cards back the way they were," Buchanan told him.

"You got quick eyes." Conrad shook his head. "Everyone to his own. I wouldn't of rode back the way you and the sheriff did for a million dollars."

"Uh-huh. It's knowin' how and when,"

18

Buchanan said. The little man was a puzzlement. It took all kinds of nerve to run a blazer in any card game in the West. There was no sign of a weapon beneath Conrad's loose jacket.

Amsy Burke put it in words. "Cole's still alive. He must know where and when."

"A man's got to live," pronounced Sheriff Lee heavily. "One way or another, it ain't easy."

Coco said, "That El Diablo was easy. Too easy. They figured to get us down there and cheat us. They figured it from the start."

"They oughta have a term in Yuma Prison," said Amsy Burke. He was drinking whiskey with his beer. "It'll cure you or kill you."

Buchanan disagreed. "It ain't a cure. I seen too many come out of jail and go from bad to worse."

"Punishment," said Lee. "That's all it is."

"Take your choice and pay the price," Amsy Burke said. "Not that I think men should be treated like they are over yonder. It's purely brutal, the heat and all."

"It's a federal prison," disclaimed Lee. "My little old jail's as comfortable as home."

"You don't feed as good as home," said Amsy Burke.

Buchanan mopped his neck. Coco's face was gleaming with sweat. Sheriff Lee arose and said, "Early's the morn. See you boys tomorrow."

He departed. Cole Conrad said, "It's been a hard day on a city man."

When the small man had left, Buchanan asked, "Amsy, how well do you know him?"

"Cole Conrad? Few years ago we met up in Tucson. He's got itchy feet. Like most gamblers, I reckon."

"You trust him?"

"As much as you can trust anybody." Burke was beginning to slur his words. "He sided me once in a saloon fight." He chuckled. "Swiped a gun from one of the galoots was raisin' hell."

"I note he don't carry a weapon."

"Strange little cuss. Never says where he came from, where he's goin'. But he did a good job for us today."

"He'd better stay out of Mexico for awhile. They got good memories down there."

"Cole's smart."

"Uh-huh," said Buchanan. "Well, I'm for bed. See you in the mornin'. Got to look in on Nightshade, see he's taken care of."

"Reckon I'll have another toddy before I turn in."

Coco followed Buchanan onto the street. He said "You got your suspicions of that Conrad, ain't you?"

"Just curious," said Buchanan. "He's mighty good with his hands. Too good."

"So's Luke Short, and he's your friend."

"Uh-huh." But his sixth sense had taken over. He had survived on the frontier for twenty years because of his instinctive preknowledge of trouble. He had been up and down the trails, he had hunted and fished in the mountains. The high plain of New Mexico, around Silver City and Santa Rita, were his stamping grounds, but he knew all the terrain of the Southwest, and a good deal of the Northern Plain, and the Rocky Mountains from California to Canada. He had spent much time in Mexico. He had been East to the big cities, and found them not to his taste. He had, as they said, seen the elephant, and now he was past thirty years of age and always seeking peace and quiet.

Coco Bean was his closest friend. The black bare-fist champion prizefighter of America would be champion of the world if allowed to fight a white man in the East. Indeed, the one man Coco had never defeated at fisticuffs was Tom Buchanan.

And Buchanan had always managed to evade this issue. There were two reasons. First, he would not in any way hurt Coco. Second, he was not about to take on the tough black man in a fair, stand-up boxing bout. It was not that he was afraid; he simply knew that to defeat Coco would diminish Buchanan in his, Coco's, own eyes. To lose would damage the fine edge of their relationship. Buchanan had learned much of the inner workings of man's mind in his travels.

There were few pedestrians on the wide street of Yuma, and no vehicles. Night-time had not improved the weather. It was still hot and muggy and no breeze relieved the tedium. The moonless night was dark as pitch. They moved, two shrouded, huge figures, toward the tiny light outside the stable. Buchanan never saw the other figure across the street. He sensed that it was there and shoved Coco out of the way the instant the light shone upon them. A shot sounded.

He snapped, "The hotel. Check Conrad's room."

His little Derringer was out of the belt buckle, almost concealed in his fist. He was zigging and zagging his way toward the spot from which had come the attack. He found himself between a general store and a house without lights. He crouched at the entry to the alleyway and waited, listening. He heard the sound of running footsteps across back lots.

He knew the uselessness and recklessness of pursuit in the dark, the way unknown to him. He walked back across the street and into the livery stable.

Nightshade, awakened by the sound of the shot, was fretful. Buchanan spoke to him reassuringly, gave him a small measure of oats, then started back to the hotel.

Coco was waiting for him on the verandah. They sat for a moment, whispering.

"Conrad's in his room," said Coco.

"You sure?"

"Woke him up. Told him there was a gun loose in the streets. He says he's scared of guns, just like me."

"Conrad's too good to be true," Buchanan said. "It must've been one of those border gunnies who were at the fight. We'll never know."

"Don't want to know," said Coco. "Want to get out of this town soon as possible or even quicker."

"We'll buy you a horse tomorrow," Buchanan promised. "Head north and into decent country. We'll take some time to fish and lay around awhile."

"Just what I had in mind," said Coco. His hatred of firearms was ingrained: he would never hunt, excepting for food when needed. But he loved to fish. "We'll go to New Mexico, right?"

"Right," said Buchanan, not entirely convinced.

He had an uneasy feeling that they would not go to New Mexico in peace.

2

BUCHANAN awoke with the dawn. His body felt sticky. The water he washed with was lukewarm. He changed into clean underwear, found a checkered shirt in his duffel and donned his boots with some difficulty. He tiptoed down the stairs and went out the back door. He made his way to the alley from which the shot had come in the night.

There was no trouble picking up tracks in the dust; the boots had been high-heeled and somewhat run over. He followed them to the edge of town. There had been a horse waiting. His guess had been correct: the bushwhacker had come from below the border. He had headed back in that direction after his aborted attempt at murder and robbery.

A restaurant was opening its doors for early birds when he walked down the street. He went in and ordered a half-dozen eggs, a rasher of bacon, fried potatoes, hot cakes with plenty of butter and syrup. It had been a few days since he had been able to sit at a table and relax and eat his fill. Until now he hadn't realized how hungry he had been.

The girl who waited on him possessed dimples. She was neat and clean and shapely. She smiled and asked, "You staying in town, Mr. Buchanan?"

"Nope," he told her. "How do you stay so cool-lookin'?"

"I was born here," she said. "My pappy was one of the early settlers. He ran a ferry over the river until he died."

Buchanan said, "And then the railroad came."

"It came after he died." She was solemn for a moment, then the smile returned. "Us natives, we keep the heat inside us, I reckon."

Buchanan asked, "How did you know my name?"

"Because word gets around fast when there ain't much else to do," she said. "You going to visit the prison?"

"Why do you ask?"

"Everyone does. People come to see how awful it is. And some come to try and find out where Rube Farnum buried the stolen money."

"I didn't know he got to bury his loot."

"He says he didn't. He says it's gone on the wind. Nobody believes him."

"Uh-huh." It was a thing to consider. Rube Farnum was a remarkable man. He was a great liar, yet he had his points. Buchanan had known him slightly and had always thought him as dangerous as he was quiet and polite.

"It does a girl good to see a man eat like you," the girl said admiringly.

He watched her go back to the kitchen. He ate slowly. Coco came in and sat beside him and the girl was just as nice to him as she was to Buchanan. Too many times Coco had been snubbed or insulted; too many times it had been necessary for Buchanan to remind people that all men are created with equal opportunity and rights.

Amsy Burke came in, eyes red and

28

swollen, but merry as usual. Behind him came Cole Conrad, like a shadow, a man not noticeable in a crowd.

Burke's voice was a croak. "Mary Jane, coffee for a poor sufferin' soul. My mouth feels like the inside of a wrangler's glove."

The waitress said, "You just as sick as if you didn't do it to yourself, Amsy." She brought steaming coffee. "Think you can eat?"

"I gotta. They don't feed us much better than the prisoners over yonder."

When the girl had left Buchanan said, "That's the most cheerful critter I've seen in Yuma."

"Everybody's friend," said Burke. "Good as gold, too. Nobody fools around with Mary Jane Brown."

"Plain name for a pretty gal," said Buchanan. He drank coffee, his appetite diminished if not fulfilled. "Best we get over and visit before noon. Got to buy a horse and mosey along today."

"I'll be with you soon as I can make it," said Burke. "Hangovers is somethin' I live with."

"Yuma's a good place to sweat it out," said Coco.

Buchanan said, "Amsy, why don't you quit today and ride out with Coco and me? We'll find you somethin' to do in the high country."

Burke swallowed scalding coffee, wiped his eyes and shook his head. "Nope. I got me a federal job, and it's safe. That's what I need, somethin' safe."

Mary Jane reappeared with a platter heaped with scrambled eggs, crisp bacon, warm bread and butter. She plumped it down and stood with a hand on hip, smiling. "Amsy's hangover mornin'."

Amsy helped himself. Cole Conrad waited, amused, then took what was left, evidently well satisfied. Mary Jane watched Burke manfully begin the meal, winked and retreated.

Buchanan asked, "There's still a ferry workin'?"

"Her pa gambled it away," said Burke between mouthfuls. "He was a happy son, but he couldn't resist a bet."

"The Colorado's a treacherous stream,"

said Buchanan. "I'll take the Gila, the way it twists and turns and never gets too rough for a man to try."

"The great river of the West," said Burke.

Buchanan found himself watching Conrad. The man's hands seemed no different from the ordinary. They were large but not extraordinarily so; the fingers were long, but not of extra length. He had a small mouth framed by a wispy mustache. He lacked color, yet there was color in him, Buchanan felt.

Finally Burke said, "I've had all I can eat. Let's go and turn me in, huh?"

Buchanan said, "Uh-huh. We're more'n ready."

"You ain't wearin' a gun, are you?"

"Never do, not in town. Unless I got business."

"They won't let weapons in the jail, of course. Even on the rock pile, some of them might go for it. That's the way Yuma gets to 'em. Farnum tried it once, with a fake he made outa soap and stuff."

"I s'pose he got solitary for that," said Buchanan.

"In Yuma it's a bad hole," Burke said seriously. "Black and tiny. Bread and water. But Farnum, he took it good. He's an odd one, Farnum."

"I recollect," said Buchanan. "Odd and smart."

Customers were entering the restaurant. Buchanan sought Mary Jane and paid for the breakfast. She gave him her bright smile and curtseyed when he added a dollar to the total.

"Thank you, sir," she said. "Every little bit helps."

"You'll make it out of here," he told her.

The others followed him onto the street. It was already too hot. They walked northward on Gila Street. The prison was built into the rocks of the bluff which overlooked the Colorado River, corner of Penitentiary Avenue and Prison Lane. There were hundreds of miles of desert in every other direction.

Burke said, "They pay the Injuns fifty

dollars a head to bring 'em back, but we've had breaks. Anybody'll try to get out of here."

He was half-bragging, half-apologizing, Buchanan thought. The adobe walls of the prison were broken by an ornamental iron gate wide enough to permit a wagon to pass through. Many a corpse had been borne beneath its arch to the cemetery on the bluff above the river.

The guard on the gate said, "You're late, Amsy."

"Meet my friends," said Burke, easily. He introduced Buchanan, Coco and Conrad.

"You got your usual snakebite headache? I need a drink more'n a calf needs its ma."

Conrad spoke up. "Here. Brought a bottle along. Take it. Keep it."

"Hey, thanks," said the guard. He quickly stowed away the pint. "Nobody's got a gun, huh?"

"All clean," said Burke.

They entered the prison, Conrad bringing up the rear, exchanging a last word with the grateful guard. There was a cellblock on the left, twenty compartments cut out of the rocky hill.

"The snake den," Burke said. "Notice the rings in the floor. Believe it or not, they're to keep the bad *hombres* from fightin' each other. Men go loco in there."

"I have no doubt," said Buchanan. The place was gloomy and filthy.

"That ain't nothin'. Over yonder is the bad place. Cells ain't big enough for a child. Farnum was in there after he tried to break out."

"Where is he now?" All the cells were full. The men were deeply tanned but none looked physically fit. Prison food. Buchanan found it hard to look at them.

"The rock pile," said Burke, leading the way. "Never did find out what they do with the little ones made out of big ones. They cart 'em away. Make roads, maybe, although there are damn few good roads."

"Roads to the desert? What use?" asked Coco. "Now you got the railway people gone to California on it."

There was a turret, and Buchanan saw

the snout of a Gatling gun protruding and a man on watch, who waved down at Burke. The man was exposed except for a roof against the sun. It was a job Buchanan would not have liked.

He had sent a few men to jail in his time. One was a millionaire. The very notion of a prison made him uncomfortable. Burke was leading them to the rock pile, conveniently located so that the Gatling gunner oversaw each movement of every man.

The convicts wore leg irons. Buchanan could see the scars, bright red on the newer arrivals, glazed with callus on the others. There were black men, Indians and one Chinaman. Then there was Farnum. He worked at the end of the line. The guard gave them a cadence, so that the heavy sledges went up and came down in rhythm.

Burke said, "Okay, Dan, how about a little time? Got some people here."

The guard named Dan had the look of one who enjoyed his work. He was beetle-browed and hard-mouthed. Reluctantly he gave the order to take a rest. The convicts stood, shoulders humped, eyes hopeless but still curious, fixed upon Buchanan and the others.

Dan said, "They're plumb lazy today. Thinkin' of gettin' out the ninetails."

"Oh, that ain't necessary," said Burke. "Farnum!"

He was a medium-sized man, with remarkable shoulders and arms, all rippling muscle. His face was ordinary, excepting for the eyes, which did not have the haunted, discouraged sheen of the others on the chain gang. He seemed to be at all times poised, like a puma, Buchanan thought, ready to pounce. Yet he was shackled, helpless.

Buchanan said, "Farnum. Sorry to see you in here."

The smile was pleasant, the voice low and husky but easy. "Not a good place, Buchanan."

"You makin' it?"

"Oh, I'll get out of here." He shrugged.

Dan, the guard, said, "You'll rot first, you bastard."

"Dan don't like me," Farnum said "Funny thing, I'm like you, Buchanan. I'm a peaceable man."

"You kilt that teller," said Dan.

Farnum shrugged. "He drawed on me," he said.

Buchanan asked, "Anything I can send you?"

"A gun and some keys." The smile broadened.

Chains rattled as the other convicts moved. The guard wheeled, his eyes sweeping up and down the line. Buchanan felt tension.

Amsy Burke said, "I'll bring him anything you send, Tom."

"He will, too," said Farnum. "He's a decent man. Not like this other buzzard."

Dan swung his rifle around. He was the only armed man in the prison, except the guard with the Gatling gun. For a moment Buchanan thought he was going to shoot. He stepped forward, knocking up the barrel of the gun.

It was a mistake, he knew at once. Cole Conrad was standing next to Farnum. In one swift motion he handed over a .45 Colt.

Farnum seemed to shoot without aiming. The man at the Gatling gun fell forward, tumbled from his perch, descended with flying arms and legs to the ground, where he lay quite still.

The Colt came around. The next shot barely missed Buchanan. It plowed into the chest of the guard named Dan.

Farnum said, "Now everybody keep real quiet. I don't want to hurt anybody."

"You just killed two men!" cried Amsy Burke.

"Them two don't count," said Farnum.

Cole Conrad was producing keys, from his hair, from inside his collar, from his shoes. He bent and unlocked the shackles after two tries. Farnum stepped loose, gingerly bending his ankles, restoring circulation.

"Okay, cousin. Now the rifle. And we'll need ammunition. Follow me."

He backed off toward the armory. The other men on the chain gang screamed at him. He paused.

He said, "Turn 'em all loose, cousin. It'll give them a heap of tracks to follow."

Conrad obediently released the others. They started for the gate, stopped in their tracks, looking fearfully at Farnum.

"Cousin gave the guard some powerful booze," said Farnum. "He'll be asleep. Warden's gone fishin', remember? Otherwise you take your chances on the people inside."

They ran for the gate. Farnum said, "Buchanan, Coco, Amsy, you follow me to the armory. Remember, I don't want to hurt none of you, but I ain't stayin' here, not now."

Pure fury shot from him, from his eyes, his entire bearing. He stared at them for a moment of precious time. Buchanan then felt the power of the man, the immense drive that was in him.

At the prison armory there was another guard, sleeping. Farnum ignored him, directing Conrad as to which case he wanted open, which ammunition to select. He chose .44s—both rifle and revolver, so that the ammunition was interchangeable.

He was as cool as a man could be under any circumstances.

Satisfied, he said, "Sorry about this. But you boys will have to sample the dungeon block. Can't have you on my heels, you know."

They started, single file, under his command. Buchanan's mind went around and around. He knew better than to make a move at this moment. The allegedly peaceable Farnum would kill at the least demonstration. He whispered to Coco, "Easy. Do as he says."

Conrad had keys for everything. Never had anyone engineered a jailbreak with more despatch, with better planning and timing, Buchanan thought. He entered the tiny cell, which could scarcely contain his bulk.

Conrad locked him in, whispering, "Sorry. Has to be."

"You're not tough enough for this," Buchanan returned. "It'll be a real hard trip from here on out."

"Rube will manage."

Coco went obediently into his cell.

Amsy Burke was next. Conrad was close to him as he opened the door. Suddenly the one-armed man grabbed the small man by the throat and held him in a bearlike embrace.

Conrad howled. Amsy swung him between Farnum and his own body. "Drop the gun, Rube. I got your cousin."

Farnum again fired offhand. The bullet grazed Conrad's ear. It struck Amsy Burke in the side of the head where it was barely exposed. His grip loosened. He sagged. He tried to speak and could not. He went down, dying.

Farnum said, "I hated to do that. Remember, Buchanan, I didn't want to do it. I know you'll be after me. I oughta kill you, too. But you did like I said. And— you'll never bring me in. Never."

Conrad, choking, went ahead. The two of them walked toward the gate. Buchanan could not see the way, but he knew they would make it to the outside world. There was no doubt in his mind.

There was nothing to do but wait. Coco called to him and he said, "Just sit quiet,

41

pardner. There'll be a hell of a lot to explain. But any warden goes fishin' is also goin' to have a lot to tell the bosses upstairs."

"I can't get over that li'l fella Conrad," Coco said in wonderment.

"I can't get over seein' Amsy go down," Buchanan said in a low voice. "Amsy was a good man."

"That Farnum, he kills people like they was ants. He purely steps on 'em," said Coco. "I thought we was goners."

"We could have been." Farnum was a strange one, all right. Prison had done certain things to the man. He would not last long on the outside. But before he gave up many would die, Buchanan knew. There was no way to prevent it.

And he would be a target for this escapee, this convict with the ice in his blood. Because he could never forget Amsy Burke's desperate move. He had thought of the same maneuver and discarded it as useless. Amsy had stepped in, regardless of the odds. Amsy had paid the price that Buchanan would have paid.

Therefore Amsy must be avenged. There was a code and this was part of it: you did not see a friend murdered and do nothing about it.

He settled down in vast discomfort to await release by someone with a key. Someone not nearly as clever with keys as Cole Conrad.

3

BEHIND an outhouse, concealed from view, Cole Conrad shed his loose coat, removed his boots and stripped off an outer pair of pants. Now he was attired in tight Levis and a work shirt. From a pocket of the coat he produced a soft hat, which he extended to Rube Farnum.

"Boots in the saddlebag. I think I covered everything," he said meekly.

Shedding the filthy prison garb, Farnum replied, "Cousin, you're a wonder. Ma always said you were the bright one of the family."

"I got my tricks. You're the smart one." He tossed keys into a mesquite bush. He said, "We go down the back way. The horses are ready, I bought 'em yesterday."

"Buyin' is always smarter than stealin'," Farnum said.

"The ferry leaves at ten-thirty. We just about got enough time."

"Yeah. The ferry. If they ain't coverin' it by then."

"They won't be. Not unless somebody heard the shots."

"I doubt they heard." Farnum frowned. "Sure hated to kill Amsy Burke. He's been real good to me."

"You killed a couple of others," said Conrad without expression. "Reckon they needed it, huh?"

"They went straight to hell."

"Yeah, I expect. We better get goin', now. Follow me."

He knew the back way. They ranged down, unobserved by the hot, preoccupied residents of Yuma. They came to the livery stable. They sauntered in and Conrad spoke to the boy. "Got our horses saddled?"

"Yes, sir."

There were three of them, the most solid mounts he could pick out. He was no great judge of horseflesh, but he knew enough from his upbringing on the farm in East Kansas not to be deceived. Farnum looked and approved.

They had played together as boys. The farm had not been hardscrabble; neither had it been very fertile. The two of them had different interests even then, but it had been harder on Cole, since he was not muscular. He was wiry and strong enough, but there was lacking in him the physical prowess and ferocity of his cousin Rube. He had always been the follower. But his prestidigitation had often enabled them to escape punishment. He could take pride in that fact.

Not that Rube was a bully nor an unkind person. His generosity and respect for certain conventions were well known. Even when he had gotten into trouble, people had thought of him as one gone astray rather than as a born thief and brawler. There was a strange gentleness in his nature. It came from their grandparents, Conrad thought, good people, church-going, originally from Virginia.

Farnum was looking at Nightshade in

his stall. "That's Buchanan's horse. If I had the guts I'd shoot him."

"Nobody can ride him exceptin' Buchanan."

"I seen an Apache try to steal him once. That Injun almost got rolled on."

"They'll be after us, Buchanan and that big black."

"You got to expect that. I know Buchanan pretty good."

"But we got a start, and we got your plan."

"Best get goin'," said Farnum. He took one more glance at Nightshade, fingered the revolver in his belt, smiled and shook his head.

Again they went the back way. At the rear door of the restaurant they paused.

Farnum said, "I don't have to tell you. No rough doin's."

"Course not."

They went into the kitchen. The place was empty excepting for Mary Jane Brown.

She said, "Hello, Mr. Conrad. You need somethin'?"

"We need you, Mary Jane." Farnum had produced his revolver.

The girl's eyes opened like saucers. "Me? You're foolin', aren't you?"

Farnum said in his pleasant, husky voice, "We ain't about to harm you none, ma'am. We just need you for awhile."

"Are you gone completely loco?" Alarm rose into her eyes.

"It's just we got to get clear of Yuma. Over the river. You see, I'm Rube Farnum. Cole, here, he's my cousin. I just broke jail, and if you don't mind, we're in a hurry."

She said, "Why, I—you can't—the sheriff and everyone will be after you."

Farnum said, "That's the exact idea, Miss Brown. With you along, we got a bit of protection. Everybody in this burg likes you, so Cole tells me."

She gazed from one to the other. She could not find words.

Conrad said, "I seen you come to work in pants. You got them handy, you better put 'em on quick."

"It might be hard goin' for awhile," said

Farnum, patiently explaining. "Don't worry, girl, we ain't the kind to harm you. We just need protection."

She said, "I change—in the other room."

"We won't watch. But don't yell nor nothin', please," said Farnum. "I don't want you hurt in no way."

The soft threat struck home. She looked at him, seeing the killer in him for one illuminating moment. She went abruptly into the small storeroom. She changed into Levis, boots and a man's shirt she sometimes wore when riding. She was partially stunned. She saw a pencil and pad on which she sometimes noted down large orders at the tables. She scribbled hastily, "Farnum and Conrad got me." It was all she dared take time to do with the pair of them waiting in the kitchen. She came out and faced them.

"We got a nice easy horse for you. Now we go to the ferry, see? They know you there. You and cousin, here, you go aboard without fuss. Like it's a pleasure trip, see? Then I come on, and then we cross the river."

She said, "You can't get far, the Rangers and Sheriff Lee and the whole country will be after you."

"We'll get there. And we'll turn you loose soon as we can," Farnum promised. "Now just get goin', please."

As in a dream she responded to the gentle voice. She mounted the sorrel they had provided. She knew horses: she was a Western girl. They rode the back way, then across to the ferry. There was a Conestoga aboard, and old Zeke was about to cast off when they arrived. He smiled at Mary Jane and held the flat-bottomed, sturdy boat. The three of them came aboard and paid the fee. Zeke was near-sighted, ageing, a man to mind his own business. Farnum gathered them together in the prow and waited as the ferry slowly made its snail pace across the Colorado.

Mary Jane said, "California will be informed. It's not easy to get away in California. I've been there on rides."

Farnum said, "You might as well know.

50

We ain't goin' into California for a long stay."

She thought about that for a moment. "You're goin' to double back? Then you got all Arizona and New Mexico lookin' for you."

"Let 'em look." Farnum was actually cheerful.

Conrad explained, "He's got it all figured out in his mind."

"Had plenty of time to figure," Farnum told her. "Breakin' rocks, sittin' in that hot cell, a man has to think to stay sane, like. You know?"

"I can imagine." She found herself conversing with these soft-spoken, mild-seeming men as though they were acquaintances from the restaurant. Which Cole Conrad was, when she thought about it. She knew about Rube Farnum. People talked about him a lot, how he had stood up under the rigors of the prison, how he was strangely gentle. "You two are cousins?"

"That's right. Our mothers were sisters," said Farnum. "Took a bit of time

51

for Cole to figure the way into the prison, collect enough money and keys and all that." He reached into the pockets of the coat which Conrad had worn and took out bunches of keys. He dropped them into the river. "He's a great one for takin' pains. He don't make many mistakes, Cole don't."

"I'd be dead long since if I did."

Farnum was walking toward the Conestoga, which was patched and dilapidated. Mary Jane glanced at the river, estimating the current. She was a strong swimmer.

Conrad said, "Don't do it. He'd be real upset if you did."

"He wouldn't hurt me."

Conrad sighed. "You might's well know. He killed three men gettin' out. All guards. He killed Amsy."

"I don't believe you."

"Sooner or later you'll find out. This is just a warnin' to you. Don't cross him."

"But you—you wouldn't kill anyone."

Conrad smiled. "So far I ain't. But he's my cousin. When we were boys, he was the one protected me. Back there in

Kansas, it was mean. People and country, all mean. Only Rube was decent to me. So you can't tell what I'll do."

She watched Farnum make his way, limping. She was confused. She had seen bad men come and go in Yuma. None resembled this pair in any fashion. They were indeed strange. She wondered about Buchanan, and if they had hurt him or the black prizefighter. She decided it was better not to ask. She had a strong will to survive. She must, she realized, obey them, praying that the promise not to harm her was meant for truth.

Farnum was examining the wagon. The driver was an emaciated man of middle age. His faded wife sat beside him, and a covey of unkempt children stared over their shoulders.

"Comin' from Kansas?" he asked.

"Texas," the man said, all the weariness in the world in his voice. "Broke down six times. Got folks in Los Angeles. Got a job promised. If we make it."

"You got mountains or a desert or both to cross."

"We made it this far. Got food. There'll be people along the way. There's always good people." The man's faded eyes sparkled with hope. "We been helped by others. God's been good to us."

"*Vaya con Dios.*" Farnum turned abruptly away. His face was stony, as though he was looking far away—or within himself. He came to where Cole was rooting into saddlebags.

Mary Jane said in surprise, "Why, that's bread and meat from the restaurant. I never saw you take that."

"His specialty," Farnum told her. "Quick hands. He always had the quick hands."

Conrad said, "Might's well eat now. Have to hustle when we get off the ferry."

They ate. Mary Jane was surprised at her appetite. She had no illusions about the danger she was in, but the calmness of the two men kept her from panic. The old rig moved slowly across the river.

Farnum gestured toward the wagon. "That's the way our folks come across back in the Forties."

"Kids and all," said Conrad. "But we wasn't born then."

"I know." Farnum chewed, swallowed. "How much cash you got, cousin?"

"Not much after buyin' the horses."

"Got a tenner?"

"Well—" He produced in his fashion, as if by magic, a ten-dollar gold piece. Farnum took it, went back to the wagon.

He said, "Take this. May not do you any good. On the other hand it might just make a difference."

The driver asked, "Why you doin' this, stranger?"

"You asked the good Lord to help. So he sent this along." Farnum laughed heartily, for the first time since he had escaped.

The man said solemnly, "The good Lord will repay you for this. I thank you in His name."

"Just take care." Farnum waved at the children and returned to the prow of the ferryboat. He winked at Mary Jane. "The Lord has strange ways sometimes now, don't He?"

She said, "I got my own notions about the Lord and how He works."

Farnum said, "Reckon we better mount up. We're gettin' close to shore and in case anybody did get loose, I'd like that wagon between me and them."

They got into the saddles. Farnum paused a moment to shorten Mary Jane's stirrups so that they were more comfortable. The ferry nosed into the landing place and they rode off, turning north, following the bend of the river.

There was a place where the current slackened, Mary Jane knew from excursions she had made during her years in Yuma. It was easy for her to deduce that, having led pursuit to the ferry, Farnum was doubling back.

She asked, "Ain't you scared of the Rangers and all them who'll be lookin' for you?"

"Like I say, let 'em look. I know the Gila country better'n they do. Better'n any man."

"How about Buchanan?" asked Conrad suddenly. "He's the most dangerous. I seen him in action. And Amsy Burke was his friend."

"Buchanan knows a heap. But New Mexico, the high country, that's his bailiwick," Farnum replied. "And anyway, they ain't goin' to come too close whilst we got this lady. They don't want to hurt her."

"Not Buchanan. Not Yuma people. But those Rangers and the bounty-hunters that'll be swarmin' for the reward, they won't give a hoot."

"If we get lucky as we have been so far, they won't never get a look at us."

Mary Jane demanded, "How far are you goin' to take me?"

"That'll depend," said Farnum. "That'll depend on how quick your friend Buchanan gets outa that cell and on the trail."

"He won't find our trail right off," said Conrad.

"You think not?"

"How could he? Us doublin' back and all. By the time he gets to the Gila he'll have to guess. And even if he guesses right we'll be long gone."

"Don't count on Buchanan not figurin' us out," Farnum said. "Don't count that he will. But don't bet against him. This ain't a card game where you control the deck, Cousin."

"I know. But the way we got it figured—"

Farnum nodded at Mary Jane. "Just keep it all under your hat for now."

"Sure, Rube. Sure enough. You're right."

Mary Jane wondered. They were cousins. Conrad had engineered the jail-break. He seemed much the more educated; he seemed to have all the savvy he needed. And yet there was not an instant's doubt who was the boss. It was Farnum.

She concentrated on riding, obeying each order she was given. She had no great confidence in their promises not to hurt her. Still, they were extraordinary men, both of them. She summoned all her courage and went on and on toward the

58

conjunction of the Gila River, that winding, mysterious stream that started high in the mountains and wandered like a lost pilgrim for its entire length. It was the river of the Navajos and the Apaches, and she began to feel a slight fear, now that she thought of the Apaches.

4

THE lack of air was the worst of it, Buchanan thought. It seemed ages that he had been in the dank, close confines of the cell. Occasionally he spoke to Coco, but there seemed little to say. His mind was on poor Amsy Burke, lying dead. Already he was thinking about Rube Farnum and in which direction he would head and how long the chase might take.

There were voices outside. Guards from the far reaches of the prison had discovered the bodies. Evidently Farnum had known the whereabouts of all the keys and had absconded with them. Buchanan answered to calls from strange voices. Then Sheriff Jake Lee arrived and with him the local smithy, who seemed also to be the locksmith.

Then there was the high wail of the warden returning from his fishing trip. He was a man in trouble. Jake Lee castigated him in no uncertain terms.

Still, Buchanan suffered in the coffin-like cell. He had been in jails before, in his time up and down the frontier, but never had he experienced anything like this. He wondered how Farnum had endured for five and a half years.

Finally they were working on the lock. He inhaled deeply, wiping sweat from his face. Jake Lee spoke reassuringly, and he answered in kind. Still, he seethed inside with the happenings of the day. Three men were dead, and Buchanan had not been able to lift a hand in defense. He felt guilty, as though he had been, however unwittingly, a party to it all.

The lock grated, the door opened. Blinded by the hot, afternoon sun, Buchanan walked into the prison yard. Half-blinded, he saw Jake Lee and a florid man who babbled words that were meaningless.

Jake said, "Warden Browning. He's a mite upset."

Buchanan nodded. The smithy was

working on the cell in which Coco sweltered. There were three inert bodies beneath pieces of sailcloth. He went to them, lifted the coverlets from the faces of each dead man. He looked long at Amsy Burke's features, twisted in his last agony.

Jake said, "I got the dogs out. Deputized a posse. Seems Farnum was headed for the ferry. If they get into California there'll be law waitin' on 'em. Got the telegraph wires burnin'."

Warden Browning said, "The governor will be wild. He'll call out the guard. I know he will. This is a terrible thing."

Buchanan ignored him. "You think they'll hit for California, Jake?"

"Nope."

"Me neither."

"The dogs'll help whichever way."

"Farnum will know about the dogs. He's been planning this for years, him and that slick cousin of his."

Jake Lee nodded. "Sure enough. It was the smartest I ever heard of. Y'know, Farnum was never a killer. That cashier, he went for a gun before he got it."

Buchanan again wiped an arm across his face. "You ever spend any time in one of those cells?"

"Not me."

"It'd give you an idea what makes a killer out of a man," Buchanan said. "Either he dies, or he turns bad—real bad."

The sheriff nodded. "See what you mean. I got to run now. There's a heap of convicts spread out in the country. Got to help round up as many as I can before they get outa my jurisdiction. You'll be wantin' to know about Farnum."

"I'll be wantin' to know."

The warden could not stop talking. Buchanan had no desire to add to the man's troubles. He was himself a fisherman. He understood the urge for the peace of field and stream. Coco emerged from his cell, his eyes round and wide. They walked toward the gate, leaving the prison employees to their own devices.

Coco said, "You know, Tom, I never was a slave."

"I know."

"But my pappy was. Settin' in there, I thought of what it must've been like. Slave quarters, punishment, all that."

"I thought of a lot of matters like that," Buchanan told him.

"Then I thought of us and how we keep goin'. And how when somethin' bad happens, we always get ourselfs into it. And we got to go on."

"Yes. We got to go on," said Buchanan.

"Reckon we better eat somethin' and be started."

"Reckon we had."

They walked toward the restaurant full of dark thoughts, not speaking further. Catching Farnum would be another of the self-imposed tasks of which Coco had spoken. It would not, Buchanan thought, be the easiest nor quickest of their adventures. He did not relish a manhunt, but Coco was right. "We got to go on."

A man came running from the restaurant. He panted, "Buchanan? You don't know me, but I own the eatery. Look here!"

He thrust a piece of paper at them.

Buchanan took it. He read it. Now the gorge rose higher inside him. "They took the girl."

"That nice waitress gal?" Coco's face turned hard.

"Mary Jane Brown. The nicest young woman in this here town," said the man. "I'm Hotchkiss. Lemme fix you all some food. Lemme do anything I can do for that little gal."

Buchanan said, "You do that, Hotchkiss. Fix us grub for takin' along. We got to buy a horse. We got plans to make. And we haven't got much time."

Despite the heat, there were people in the streets now. They were all full of indignation and opinions. Buchanan and Coco pushed their way through them to the livery stable. The owner told them of the three horses he had sold. He had only a roan left, he said, but it had bottom, and bottom was what they would need for a long chase. He did not ask an exorbitant price, and the horse seemed adequate to carry Coco. Buchanan paid and they picked out a worn but sturdy saddle, adjusted the stirrups, brought Nightshade from his stall, and made ready. They rode to the hotel and tied up at the hitching rail.

The clerk was full of excitement. Buchanan asked, "Have you got a map of this country?"

"I got an Arizona map, a good one."

"How much?"

"It's yours," said the clerk. "I know who you are. And I had many a drink with Amsy Burke."

"Thanks." Buchanan took out money. "See that he has a decent burial, will you, friend?"

"The town will do that. Amsy was well liked."

Buchanan said, "Then add something to it. Whatever." He led the way upstairs. They packed their belongings and then they sat down and pored over the map.

Buchanan said, "I know part of this layout but not enough. Farnum knows it all. He's been turnin' it over in his mind for five and a half years."

"You think he won't go to Mexico or California?"

"He wouldn't have a Chinaman's chance. That's where the others will head. They'll be rounded up in no time."

There was a tap on the door. Jake Lee came into the room. He said without preamble, "They took the ferry. Old Zeke just came in to tell about it."

"They took the ferry and they didn't kill Zeke nor tie him up nor anything?"

"Just so," said the sheriff. "Funny thing."

"Funny thing is right."

"No, they doubled back all right. I got men lookin' for track. Farnum ain't all that smart. Thing is, he gave some poor folk money to go on to California."

"He did what?"

"Gave 'em a gold piece he got from Conrad."

Buchanan shook his head. "A man of many parts. A very dangerous man. It'll be hard to figure his moves."

"If he gets by—and he will—he'll

prob'ly go up the Gila a ways. It's wild, deserted country."

Buchanan said, "He'll need food. Jake, didn't somebody say the loot from that last bank robbery never was found?"

"That's right."

"Then he's headin' for it. And he knows we'll be thinkin' right along. Only one thing."

"Yeah."

"Where did he stash the loot?"

"He was loose awhile," said Jake Lee. "He damn near got away. He had time to hide it."

"Any ideas?"

"You think people ain't been lookin' for fifty thousand dollars? There was a big payroll in the bank that day."

"Would you say somewhere near Tucson?"

"I'd say that."

"And nobody's found it. So the only way to get him is to follow him until he gets to it."

"Which ain't goin' to be easy. There'll be Tucson people lookin' for him. But he could play dead for any length of time before he went to it."

"And he's the man to do it," said Buchanan. "Only one way to go about this."

"Know what you mean. Wish I could go along," said Jake. "My job is here in this county, roundin' up the others that got away. Reckon you'll be pressin' him."

"That's the story." Buchanan returned to the map. "He's got a few choices. He'll take the hard way. He's that kind."

"I pity anybody gets in his way," said the sheriff.

Coco said, "I pity him if we get to him first."

"Amsy Burke," said Jake Lee. "I know. I sure wish I could go along."

He left them.

Buchanan looked at the scribbled note left by Mary Jane Brown. Then he looked again at the map. The dead face of Amsy Burke interposed, the head broken by Farnum's bullet.

"The man said he was sorry," he said

to Coco. "Sorry he killed Amsy. Damn his soul."

"Sorry don't do it," Coco agreed. "Why did they cross the river, Tom? Smart one like Farnum, he knows it would be found out that he come back."

"He had a reason," Buchanan said. "I expect he's been in California before. They got to have more supplies. They got to have clothing. He may have had a cache across the river of some kind. Maybe Conrad planted something there. Something they needed." He returned to the map. "They won't go to the railroad, not with the girl along. Too dangerous, trying to get her into a boxcar or whatever."

"That nice little gal," Coco said. "Can't we get movin'?"

"Look at the map. See how the Gila wanders around? A great river, but I don't know the country like Farnum does. See how few towns? He'll have to hit the towns to keep going, to get food."

"Can't we just go and track him?"

"We got to know where to start."

70

Buchanan shook his head. "How far up the Gila will he go?"

"You sure he's goin' that way?"

"Not sure of anything about him. And that sneaky little cousin of his—"

"We gotta start some place."

"Uh-huh. If I had a notion as to just where that loot was hid—but since everybody seems to have looked and nobody knows." He was thinking aloud. "Coco, you're right. We got to start someplace. Might just as well be at the beginning."

"Where they come back off the Colorado?"

"Where they'll hit the Gila."

"Supposin' they don't go that way?"

"Then we'll have to start over. But Farnum, if the loot's hidden around Tucson he'll start one way, then go another. He'll try to throw us off by maneuverin'. He's got that kind of schemin' head on him."

Buchanan folded the map with care. There was a time and a place, and he had to make a choice, and he knew that which he was up against. He put the map away and got out his revolver and oiled it and put on the cartridge belt he never wore excepting when danger called. He nodded to Coco. They went downstairs, checked out of the hotel, stowed their gear upon the rigs of the horses, and mounted.

It was not in Mary Jane Brown's character to fall into prolonged despair. She had fear; it was genuine, but she was, for now, able to bury it deep within her. She rode the horse with the two men always watchful of her; she was silent as much as humanly possible; she asked no questions. She did observe.

She had been on her own since she was fifteen, which had been five years ago. Her schooling interrupted by the death of her father, she had managed to scratch out a living without the patronage of any of the men who had desired her body. Her independence was sure and serene. Still, now there was the fear. Her lack of experience with men made it worse. Yet she held it down and watched them as they watched her.

In California, after the crossing, there had been a buried something, a box and some ammunition. She did not know what was in the box but she did note, before Farnum stowed it away, that it was marked with a double X, meaning "dangerous."

They did not pause. They took her north and knew just where to recross the river, swimming the horses, so that when they came back to Arizona she knew they were making for the Gila River. She also knew of the dangers inherent upon this move, the desert ahead, the chance of running into roving bands of Indians. There were always some Apaches who were off the reservation, and word had been going about that one named "Geronimo" was a wily and dangerous leader. She had heard all this in the restaurant, all the stories of depredations across the border, murder of small ranchers and farmers, quick retreats into the wilderness. The Apache could live anywhere on nothing, people said.

She rode until nightfall, exhausted but

young and strong enough to stay with the pace set by the two men. They made camp beside the Gila where it emptied into the Colorado.

Conrad said, "Hope you're all right, Mary Jane."

She did not answer him, watching as they made a fire.

Farnum said, "She can't be all right. But she's not to come to harm. We need you, Mary Jane. I promise that when and if we don't need you, we will release you unharmed."

"Thank you," she said with deep sarcasm. Still, somehow she believed him. She did not really believe Conrad. There was something about him that alarmed her, something in the way he looked at her behind the back of his cousin.

Farnum said, "There's only one man to worry on."

"Buchanan," said Conrad. "You damn right. 'Scuse my language, Mary Jane. I seen that *hombre* in a cut. He's trouble."

"I couldn't kill him in cold blood," said Farnum. "The guards, they're animals.

74

I'm sorry about Burke, but the others got what was comin' to them. I kill nobody don't get in my way, Mary Jane."

"That's nice," she said.

"Don't be like that," he said reprovingly. "Me bein' that way can save your life."

"Nothing can save me if Buchanan finds you," she said. "You think I don't know that?"

"Buchanan'll never come close while you're with us," he replied. "He'd rather see us get away."

"But then I'd be really in your way," she told him. "If somebody besides Buchanan spots you, it'll be different."

"Just pray," he advised her.

Conrad laughed in his gentle fashion. "The Lord ain't lookin' down on us. You do the prayin', Mary Jane."

He was making coffee on one side of the fire and skillfully arranging a pan on the other. His hands were deft and swift as he produced bacon and beans from a tin. There was something about the way he handled the utensils which was fascinating to her.

Darkness came upon them. Farnum sat on a flat rock, his rifle near his right hand. She had noticed that he never made a move unless the rifle was nearby. He rubbed the scars, callused, on his ankles. The firelight etched his brooding, jagged profile against the night. "I won't feel free until we get where we're goin', get a new start. I never meant to get into robbin' banks. It was a tough life in Kansas, and it got tougher out here. You know that, Cole."

Conrad said, "It's always been tough. I was doin' fine with the cards until too many got to know me." He smiled. "If I had any luck and didn't have to cheat, I'd be up there with Luke Short. Ownin' a joint like the one he's got in Dodge. The Long Branch. That's what I wanted, a joint like the Long Branch."

"A saloon never was for me." Farnum sighed. "I don't truly know what it is I want. I seen the big cities, I worked the cattle drives. Ranchin' ain't it. I guess what I'll do is travel."

"I guess what we'll have to do is travel." It was not said in a joking manner, Mary Jane noticed. Conrad was an enigma in the shadows, watching the fire yet not close to it, able to move when he had to move. Like a puma, she thought, a gentle but still dangerous cat. Back in Yuma, he had seemed a harmless little man, overshadowed by Buchanan and Coco and big, bluff Amsy. Here on the trail he was vastly different. At least so it seemed to her in her fears.

Farnum said, "Five and a half years. Mary Jane, you don't have no notion of what it's like."

"I never robbed a bank," she told him. She was less and less afraid of Farnum. His voice was clear and soft, he seemed to dwell inside himself, scarcely glancing at her, as though she was a person, not a young woman. His manner was open—she almost thought "honest."

"You never had to," he replied. "I hope you never get to it."

Conrad's laughter was high and light. "A pretty gal like Mary Jane? Why, anyone'd hire her in a minute. If I get my saloon, she can be top lady."

"No thanks," she retorted. Farnum was holding up his hand, his face sharp and eyes intent. There was the sound of a shot. The coffee pot toppled.

Farnum dove for the girl, carrying her into the brush nearby the river. Conrad slid the other way, quick as a snake heading for cover. Mary Jane held her breath.

Farnum whispered, "Musket shot. Tell by the sound. A rifle and one of us'd be dead. Apache."

She clung to earth. He patted her shoulder and was gone, leaving her to the shelter of a fallen log. She lay there, trying to dig herself into earth, knowing of the Apaches, knowing that Geronimo's followers were mainly renegades, knowing her fate if she were captured.

She heard nothing, then birdcalls from human throats. Immediately there was a crackling of dry brush. The fire had not quite gone out. A painted face showed itself not ten feet from where she cowered.

Farnum's rifle cracked. The Apache fell across the fire, smothering it. There were two more shots. There was a weird, high yell from afar. Conrad showed himself for an instant, firing a revolver. A body crashed. Another went into the river. Then there was silence.

She lay there for what seemed an eon. The birds were silent, only the buzzing of insects relieved the vacuum. She was afraid to breathe.

Farnum spoke in her ear so that she nearly jumped out of her skin. "It's all right. But we've got to move."

Now she could smell the nauseating scent of scorched flesh of the Indian who had fallen into the fire. She said, "I—I don't know if I can make it."

"They nearly got our horses," he told her. "Just a small scouting party, but one got away. He'll report to Geronimo. We've got to leave this part of the country or the whole bunch will be after us."

Conrad appeared, always the ghost,

always nearly invisible. "Geronimo travels with eighty to a hundred bad ones. Grab up what food you can."

"We'll have to leave the Gila," said Farnum. "Maybe try for Walton. Forty-odd miles."

Conrad said, "Got to make it."

She dragged herself to her feet. She was in shock. She did not look at the dead Indian; she managed to get back into the saddle. She ached in every muscle of her body. Out of the corner of her eye she saw Farnum turning over the dead man, examining him.

"One of Geronimo's for sure," he said. "Painted up for a raid into Mexico. If we get clear they won't follow. He's real canny, that Geronimo. Fella in the prison knew him good."

"He ain't a real chief, is he?"

"Nope. Just a smart fella took over when Cochise and Victorio give up," said Farnum. He was grabbing bundles, stowing them on the horses. "Let's *vamos* pronto."

The night ride was hard. She swayed in

the saddle, nearly asleep at times, hurting at other times. She knew Walton, a tiny town, indefensible against men like Farnum and Conrad. She was slowly giving up her chances. She realized there was no escape from these two so long as they needed her. Her thoughts flashed again and again to the one man they feared. She wished and wished for Buchanan to loom upon the horizon.

Buchanan and Coco heard the shots in the distance. They had been casting around for track and nightfall had prevented them from going further. They mounted and rode. They had gone a mile when Buchanan said, "Whoa. Right here."

There was a stand of trees, grown thickly together near the Gila. They rode into the copse and dismounted. It was a dark night.

Coco asked, "What did you make out?"

"Indians. I can smell 'em. The shots were over yonder. You know Geronimo is out."

"They said he don't come this way."

"They never know where he's comin' from. He's snake-smart. The cavalry's lookin' for him over yonder. He's here."

"You sure?"

"Nope."

Coco scratched his head. "Well, if there's Injuns, you'd know. You always do."

"Been with 'em and agin 'em all my life, one time or another," Buchanan said. "Listen!"

They were riding up ahead. He could hear a wail wafted on a breeze. He led the way to the far side of the thick growth. He motioned to Coco to dismount and stay with the horses. He crept out of the woods and through the brush.

He froze. A moment later two Apaches came at him in the dark, wielding short axes. He shot one, closed with the other, dropping his rifle. He found himself matched with a muscular, quick brave whose skin was well oiled. He closed his nose against the stink and held the man's axe arm. He evaded a foot-trip well executed. He squeezed the arm in his left hand, felt the brave lose breath. He slammed hard, using his hip. When the Indian flew loose he leaped forward and kicked hard. The toe of his boot caught the side of the head of his opponent. The Indian lay like a log.

Buchanan helped himself to the axe and a long knife. He lit a taper and made sure the man was dead, his neck broken. He heard wild yells of anger ahead. He crawled on, retrieving his rifle, the Indian's weapons in his belt.

He came to the edge of a small clearing. A fire had been recently lit. He saw the bodies of three Apaches. The Apaches were furious, gesturing, demanding. They were gathered around a squat ugly leader.

It was Geronimo. He began to harangue them. Buchanan listened.

"True, we have lost brethren here. True, those who did the deed were few. True, we could overtake them. But when? Not soon enough. We go south, to Mexico."

Braves yelled at him, relatives of the dead men, Buchanan thought. Geronimo faced them, scowling, an ugly man with power in his voice and gestures.

"We go for the good of us, the People. We accept our losses. We bury our dead. But we go on to riches, slaves, guns that we need so sorely. We go to Mexico!"

The yells were diminishing. Buchanan backed off. He went back through the undergrowth and into the trees with more speed than guile.

He said, "Geronimo's whole crowd'll be coming this way."

"What happened over yonder?"

"Somebody—could've been Farnum—made a stand. We can't pick up track until daylight nohow. So we got to keep outa the way of this damn maraudin' bunch."

"How we goin' to do that?"

"We got to turn back. To the Colorado."

"Won't we lose time gettin' to Farnum?"

"I don't even know it was Farnum up there. I reckon it was. But I don't know." He was already astride Nightshade. "See if that roan of yours can run some."

It was a disappointing ending to the day. But he knew they had to get past the flank of the Apache raiders. They rode through the night, Buchanan in the lead. They were assailed by clinging brush, trees appeared like monsters in the path. They rode a devious route, seeking no trail, wanting only to avoid a show-down fight with too many Indians.

When they came at last to the river, Buchanan halted. He knelt and put his ear to the ground. Coco watched. Both horses were panting, even the mighty Nightshade. It had been a dangerous, grueling ride.

Buchanan stood up. "Can't hear them. We make a dry camp. We watch all night. In the morning we look."

"One thing. If it was Farnum up yonder he didn't have no time to cover his trail."

"Uh-huh," said Buchanan. "Here's a sandwich. Make it last. There might be a long time between meals."

"You tell me? You the hungry man."

"I'm tellin' you so I won't think too much about it myself," Buchanan said.

He munched on his own sandwich. They were silent for moments. Then Coco asked, "You run into somethin' out there?"

"Uh-huh."

"Injun?"

"Uh-huh."

Coco nodded. "I can always tell."

"Uh-huh. You sure can."

Coco said very softly, "You always git down when you got to kill somebody. I know you hate to do it. But these are bad Injuns."

"Bad, good. Sendin' a man on don't never appeal."

"It don't bother Farnum none, seems like."

"It bothered him to kill Amsy. When a man's in trouble he does what he thinks he's got to do."

"Amsy shouldn't have done what he done."

"Amsy was that kinda man."

"And he got dead for it. People with guns. I know I said it too many times. I still say it."

"And you're right. Which don't alter the facts. Without guns we'll never get to Farnum and the girl."

Coco sighed. "You handle that part. Me, just lemme get my hands on 'em."

Buchanan said, "I got the Indian with my hands and feet."

"Oh." Coco pondered. "I see what you mean."

"I know you do. And you got a right to feel like you do about guns. But whatever way, in this country at this time, we try to do what's right."

There was no more to say on the subject, and Coco knew it. They had been over the ground for years. Neither could ever convince the other. Buchanan knew that there would come a time when guns would not be worn by all. But he also felt that as long as weapons were manufactured, there would be those who would use them.

He could honestly say that Buchanan had never fought for selfish purposes. Buchanan was truly peaceable. Many a time when attacked in a bar solely because

Buchanan was so huge, or because he was Buchanan, he had turned his back. Many a punch had landed on his shoulders when it was not worthwhile to retaliate. Many a drunk he had bear-hugged and gently disposed of without harm to the attacker.

Yet he had killed too often, Buchanan thought. He had ridden up and down the frontier seeking peace, fishing, hunting, enjoying his friends. And too many times his friends had become involved in trouble and he had interposed. And generally, because of the time, because of the nature of the west it had ended in death.

He carried the scars to prove it had not been all one-sided. Even as he went to his blankets, there were twinges and aches resulting from old wounds. It was a dog-eat-dog life most of the time.

5

BUCHANAN drank the black coffee and waited for the first sign of sun. Coco ate silently, his eyes half-closed. It was going to be a clear day. Birds sang, and there were no signs of Indians. Each had spent a restless night and each was anxious to go on, yet their moves were unhurried as they made ready.

The horses, well rested, were eager and ready for a run. It took a few moments to calm them, then the pair rode for the river.

Buchanan said, "The shots came from over yonder."

"Yeah. I remember."

The river, the mysterious Gila, wound around and around. Buchanan rode warily in front, lest Geronimo had left a rear guard. Buchanan found no sign and forged onward. At last he raised a hand and Coco slowed down.

"Camp," said Buchanan.

He dismounted and looked at the fire. There were scraps of cloth and leather, and a distinct odor lingered.

"Somebody got it here," he said. "Probably Apache. They recover their dead ones."

Coco said, "You figure they attacked Farnum and them?"

"No question. See here? Plain footprints of the girl, smaller than the others. Nobody had time to cover trail."

"Indians went on south, like you said."

"Uh-huh. Farnum followed the river. But how far?"

"Reckon that's for us to find out."

Buchanan walked a few rods. He came back, nodding. "Three horses. Farnum defended real good. Apaches usually get the horses first off. Farnum's goin' around the mountain and through the pass."

Coco sat the horse. "I see the problem. We can't close in too fast because they got the little old gal."

"That's right." He bestrode Nightshade. "We'll follow track as long as we can. Then we'll have to guess."

"Guess like what?"

"A town. There's Walton."

"Ain't that the hidey place for outlaws and such?"

"That's what they tell me."

"You reckon Farnum'd be welcome there?"

"Maybe not welcome. But I don't figure anybody's goin' to give him much of an argument if he chooses to stop."

"We don't know for sure he's gone there."

"Keep ridin'."

They rode. The trail was plain enough. The fugitives had been in a hurry. The imprints were deep. Buchanan wondered if there were fresh mounts in Walton. When he found where the river swung northward, then south again, he slowed down.

He said, "They tried to cover tracks here. See where they dragged a branch?"

"Can't see a doggone thing like of that," said Coco.

"It takes a few years," Buchanan admitted. There was a path through some wooded acres, then a narrow trail. He followed it. The road widened and he knew he was heading for a town. There were a few wagon tracks and hoofmarks. Walton, he knew, was not a metropolis. It was an isolated by-station where a man could hole up while the law looked for him elsewhere.

Coco asked, "What's to prevent them from bushwhackin' us?"

"Nothin'," said Buchanan. "I aim to be careful."

They rode paralleling the narrow path as much as possible. Checking back on the tracks took time. It was almost evening by the time they had traversed to the outskirts of Walton. Buchanan glanced overhead.

The thin wire of the telegraph had been cut and was dangling. "Looks like Farnum's been down this path."

He took out a pair of pliers from his pack, mounted the pole and repaired the wire. Coco watched for signs of danger, perceived none. Buchanan climbed back to earth.

"Just in case," he said, indicating the wire. "Not that it will do any good. The whole country must be hummin' with the news of Farnum's escape. There'll be bounty-hunters and lawmen all over the place. Let's go to town."

"You don't think he'll be layin' for us there?"

"If he is, then we've found him."

"And the gal."

"And the gal," said Buchanan. "We leave the horses outside this burg. May want to get to 'em in a hurry."

Coco said, "I don't mind walkin'. It's you that hates it."

They found a convenient cul-de-sac and unbridled the horses so that they could graze. They walked toward the town, now lit by a dim and foreboding light from a couple of buildings, otherwise dark.

Walton consisted of a general store, a saloon and several dwellings scattered hither and yon, none of them prepossessing. There was little farming in the area where Geronimo roamed, and it was not cattle country. It was a desolate scene. Buchanan and Coco approached with caution.

Coco muttered, "Walton? Looks like Sinktown to me."

Buchanan headed for the general store. There was a middling man behind the counter. He had a shotgun at his side. Buchanan raised his arms.

"Just wanted to ask a question. Two men and a girl been through here today?"

"You damn betcha. You friends of theirn?"

"No," said Buchanan.

"Lawmen?" It was said in the same unfriendly fashion.

"No."

"Bounty hunters?"

"No."

"You better go down to the saloon. I had enough of strangers." He clutched the shotgun.

Buchanan asked, "How much did they take from you?"

"None of your damn business."

94

"Uh-huh. Plenty to carry them a good way." Buchanan shrugged and backed to the door. Coco held it open. They both ducked out of doors.

Coco said, "Gun every place you look. That's a mean man in there. Farnum must've scared him."

"Uh-huh," said Buchanan. "Watch that he don't come behind us. He might hate Farnum for stealin', but he don't favor us."

They walked down to the saloon. It was a small place, not clean. Buchanan looked over the batwing doors. There were a half-dozen men at the far end of the bar. He motioned to Coco to cover him and stepped quickly inside, ranging to the near end of the small, L-shaped bar. There was silence. The bartender was a grizzled, scarred veteran. He wore a star of office on his loose-hanging, soiled vest. His eyes were slanted, squinting.

Buchanan asked, "You the law?"

"Marshal Cassidy." It was a half-grunt.

"I just fixed your telegraph wire," Buchanan told him.

Marshal Cassidy jerked a thumb at one of the customers. "Al, get on down to your office. It'll be hummin'." He stared at Buchanan. "What's your business, stranger?"

"Name of Buchanan. I'm lookin' for two men and a girl."

"I don't see no badge."

"I don't wear one," Buchanan said. "It's personal." They were all half-turned toward him now. They were an unprepossessing crowd. Each wore his six-gun down where it was handy to his grasp.

Cassidy asked, "You drinkin'?"

Buchanan put a coin on the bar. "Have one yourself."

Cassidy nodded. He took a bottle from beneath the counter, placed two four-ounce glasses side by side. He lifted his, chock-full, downed it, never taking his eyes from Buchanan, proving that the booze held no chloral hydrate. Buchanan followed suit. It was surprisingly good liquor.

Buchanan said, "I'm not interested in anybody but the three I mentioned."

"Farnum," said Cassidy. "He cut the wire. I knowed him by an old handbill. Farnum and whoever."

"The girl's a hostage," said Buchanan.

"How much is the reward?"

"I wouldn't know."

"It'll be enough. Him havin' the gal wouldn't stop us if we had the news quick enough."

"Uh-huh," said Buchanan.

"You the real Buchanan?"

"Check with Coco Bean," said he, gesturing toward the door. The black man filled the frame.

"I know 'bout him. You're it, all right." Cassidy slanted his gaze around the saloon. "You got your hosses at the livery stable?"

"Farnum ran off every horse in town, didn't he?"

"How the hell would you know?"

"What would you do under the circumstances?"

Cassidy belched, poured himself another whiskey. After a moment's hesitation he filled Buchanan's glass, waved away payment. "I'll buy your hosses." He replaced the bottle beneath the bar.

"Farnum took the town." Buchanan nodded. "The store, the saloon, the whole town. Right?"

Cassidy said, "The sonofabitch stole my best hoss."

"And you want to go after him."

"And I'll get him and kill him."

"Even if it means that the girl gets hurt."

"The hell with the girl. Any floozie stands in my way can take her chances."

"The girl's not a floozie. She's a friend of mine," said Buchanan.

"That makes it tough on you." Cassidy made a careless motion with his left hand. Buchanan watched his right.

The right hand dove beneath the bar. At the same time, one of the customers went for his six-gun. Coco shouted.

Buchanan slid out his revolver. One shot went down the bar and the man who had attempted to draw howled, clutched his shoulder and fell backwards. Cassidy looked into the black muzzle, still smoking.

Coco came in like a whirlwind. Guns flew from holsters; men tumbled one upon the other like logs piled by a lumberjack. In a minute no one was armed nor left standing.

Cassidy said, "You're that Buchanan, all right. Never did see such a slick move."

"Just hand me whatever you got under there. Butt first," Buchanan said.

It was a sawed-off *greener*. Buchanan broke it, removed the shells, cracked the lock across the edge of the mahogany.

"The law," he said. "Offer a reward and some of you jaspers forget you ever saw a badge, if that *is* an honest badge you're wearin'. Now just tell me how much head start they got and we'll call it off for now."

"They got away before noon," Cassidy said. His half-closed eyes were sinister. "We'll be on the trail soon as we can get horseflesh. You better watch your back, Buchanan."

"If we hadn't been doin' just that, you might have run your blazer on us,"

Buchanan reminded him. "Now that the town's shown its colors, we'll be picking up what supplies Farnum left. You boys better mind yourselves. Me and Coco, we don't like to get into a fuss. But you see how it is."

Cassidy said, "I heard all about you, Buchanan. But I knowed Hickok in my time, and plenty like him. None of 'em ever scairt me."

"Uh-huh. Wonder you're still alive," said Buchanan. "Plenty of 'em scared me. Special when they were drunk. I'll be lookin' for you from now on. You savvy? Lookin' hard."

He motioned to Coco and they backed out of the barroom. They walked back to the general store. The owner was waiting, the gun still near his hand. Buchanan put money on his counter.

"We'll be needin' some things. Just tend to the order. Leave the gun where it is."

The man looked at the money. "You don't need to worry. I heard the shot. I heard Sandy yell. I know that howlin' voice. You come out of there alive, you pays, I give you what you need."

"Smart fella. You'll go far in business," said Buchanan.

But they were losing time and they had no idea in which direction Farnum would head next and now it was growing dark and they would have to make another camp. He felt growing unease. He had not gained a step upon Farnum and Conrad— and the girl. Mainly, as did Coco, he worried about Mary Jane Brown.

Cole Conrad opened a can of peaches and tendered them to Mary Jane. "Compliments of the town of Walton." His smile was gentle but probing. He was trying to make her feel safe, she knew. He was also moving very close to her as she ate the peaches.

Farnum said, "That was good horseflesh we picked up. They'll take us a long way, with luck."

"I like the extra pack animal with the food and stuff," said Conrad. "I hope one of them dresses fits you, Mary Jane, for when we get to town. You'll need a change by then."

She said, "I need a change now. And a bath. And a comb."

"A comb? There's a comb in the package," said Conrad. "A gal always likes to look neat and pretty, don't she?"

Farnum said sharply, "Never mind that. We've got a hell of a long, hard ride ahead. Pretty don't matter."

"It's just to get the snarls out," Mary Jane said to him.

"Pretty always counts," said Conrad with his soft, insinuating manner. He gave her the comb. He looked at Farnum, caught his cold gaze, looked quickly away, smiling.

"We got to get on come sunrise," said Farnum. "I'll stand the first watch. I got matters to puzzle out. Cole, this ain't your deal, but stay awake when you take your turn. Girl, you can sleep all night in them new blankets we got in Walton."

Conrad said, "I'll sleep. Always could. Clear conscience, I reckon." He laughed heartily at his own joke. He produced coins and made them tumble along his fingers, from pinky to the thumb, one on each hand. He made a simple gesture and showed empty palms. "Tricks to the tricky," he observed. "A man learns how to make his way. Rube, here, he got into a bind, girl. But I got him out. He's a good man. Give us a start and we'll both be good men."

He went to his gear, wrapped himself, placed his head upon a saddle blanket and turned away from the small fire. Mary Jane combed her hair, watching Farnum.

He sat near the fire, the rifle ever present at hand as though it were a part of him. He said, "It ain't true, you know. We might get away. But we'll never be good men, the kind that settles down and raises a family and all. We might could get where we don't rob any more. There's that chance. But Cole, he's got those nimble, tricky fingers. And me, I got a price on my head."

She bound up her hair in a bandanna. "You don't seem bad to me. Even now, you don't seem really bad."

103

"Thanks," said Farnum. "That's the only nice thing anybody's said to me in many a long year."

"If you let me go I could find my way back home. You don't need me anymore. You've got clean away."

He cocked an eyebrow at her. "With Buchanan after us?"

"Oh. Buchanan."

"I don't give a hoot for any of the others. They'd come in whether we had you along or not, but I'd be ready for them. But Buchanan, he's another dealer."

"I scarcely know him."

"You don't know the West like we do. Buchanan's been around since the old trail days. He's been to Dodge, to Fort Worth, he's been to Montana and Wyoming. He's been places where they still talk about him years after he's gone."

"He's awful big. I mean tall and wide."

"He's been a good target for many a backshooter. Nobody I ever heard of got him from in front, where he could see. Oh, yes. While Buchanan's on the trail, we got to hold you. With all his toughness, he'd deal for you."

She was silent for a moment. Then she asked, "Like you would?"

He turned away. "Nobody stands in my way gets off alive. I done enough hard time. Don't get thinkin' I'm a softy, Mary Jane. Don't ever think that."

"I could never think that. I lived in Yuma too long."

She went to the blankets, across the dying fire from Conrad. Farnum hefted the rifle, looked down at her, then at his cousin.

He said, "I'm goin' to take a look around. I'll be near enough."

"Good night," she said. But she could not quickly get to sleep. A hundred thoughts ran through her head. Farnum would deal for her, as he said. He could also kill her if Buchanan or whoever caught up with them refused to deal.

She twisted. The last glowing ember of the fire caught the open eyes of Cole Conrad. He was smiling at her. She turned over, not responding. She knew another danger. The seemingly quiet and meek cousin was a womanizer. She had enough experience to recognize all the symptoms. If ever Farnum relaxed his vigilance. . . .

On the other hand, Farnum was a strict disciplinarian. She remembered a school-teacher who had come to Yuma when she was younger, and her father was alive. He had been a fair man but he had made the kids toe the mark to the point of desperation. She had been miserable under the tutelage of that man. And in the end it was found that he was a secret boozer, and that he had tampered with one or two of the older girls.

Not that the girls had fought him off, she thought, chuckling to herself. She had seen it all. She had remained apart from it all. Now she was the captive of a strict killer and a tricky lady-killer. She had to laugh to keep from weeping.

In the night some time, she felt a hand on her. She started awake, clutching the blankets. Conrad was still smiling. He whispered to her, "You had chucked off the covers. I was just tuckin' you in."

She wound herself tighter in the blanket. She said, making herself seem sleepier than she was, "Thanks. Thanks—" she said, trailing off, closing her eyes. He did not touch her again that night. She lay awake, listening to the rustle of foxes, the distant howl of a coyote, the slithering of reptiles afraid of people as people were afraid of them. She had never known true misery until now. She had been able to handle every situation, including the death of her father, the lack of a mother she never knew. Now the fear within her stirred and rippled. When she did sleep it was to dream of things not quite real but certainly evil. . . .

When she awakened, Farnum was returning, rifle in hand. Conrad had coffee boiling. She closed her eyes and pretended to be asleep.

Conrad asked, "Don't you never sleep?"

"Had five and a half years to sleep," replied Farnum. "There's Indian sign."

"Close by?"

"Comin' and goin'. Not Geronimo's

bunch. Apaches come in all styles. Maybe a huntin' party."

"They're just as dangerous if they're feelin' raunchy."

Farnum said, "Speakin' of raunchy, I been noticin' how you eye the girl."

"Can you blame me?" He laughed in his gentle fashion.

"I can warn you."

"You think I'd try anything whilst we're on the run? I ain't crazy, cousin."

"You ain't exactly all there, neither. You never was. I mind Grandma sayin' as much. You and your tricks."

"Me and my tricks got you outa Yuma."

"Correct. Now me and my ways are goin' to set us free for good. That is, if you behave yourself."

Conrad paused a moment. Then he said in a low voice, "I'll behave. But if I get the chance, if it don't harm nothin', if the road's clear—I want the gal."

"That's a lot of ifs," said Farnum. "I don't see any of them ifs ahead. We got to ride, and we got to change boots in case they bring dogs, and we got to be mighty smart. And then when we get the plunder we got to make sure there's a way out. You harm that gal, and all hell won't stop them from gettin' to us. You ought to know enough about the west to figure that."

"I know enough," said Conrad. "It's just—well, she's the kind of gal I always wanted. Young, decent—if we got enough money, maybe she'd go along with us."

"You think she'd marry you?"

Conrad shrugged. "Who's talkin' about marriage? It may be Rosabelle never did get a divorce. I might still be married."

Farnum said, "Get ready to move." He drank coffee. He came to Mary Jane and touched her. She started as if she was suddenly coming awake. "Come on, girl. We got many a mile to cover."

She obeyed. It was then she began to hate the smooth, easygoing, easy-talking Cole Conrad. *A gun*, she thought, *I'll have to try and steal one of their guns. Or a sharp knife. Some kind of a weapon.* She went through the motions, dutifully ate, climbed onto the horse, and rode with them. They had stolen a wiry cayuse for the pack animal, and the pace was swift. Unaccustomed to long rides, Mary Jane was soon sore again, so that she thought even her bones ached. Fear and hatred kept her going on. She had to wrench her gaze away from Conrad's supple, clever hands, imagining them pawing at her. She had no idea where they were, where they were headed. She was at the bottom, she thought, deep in the pit.

Buchanan and Coco came to the campsite. It was near dark again. The horses needed water and rest. They alighted and stirred the ashes of the fire. They were cold.

Buchanan said, "They got a good start, and they're movin' faster than I thought possible."

"Too fast for me." Coco did not enjoy long, hard journeys aboard a horse.

Buchanan said, "Might as well make a fire. But keep it low. Can't tell if there's bounty hunters or worse in this country. I'll make a *pasear*."

He walked a circle. In the dusk he

found Farnum's tracks. He followed them, knowing the man had been wary, careful. He picked up the Indian sign. He followed it past the campsite. He saw the trail of the three horses. The Apaches had also spotted them, he knew. It seemed as though the Indian party was stalking the escapees and the girl.

He came back to camp glum and discouraged. "It's plain which way Farnum started. But it's too dark to know which way he's goin'. And there's Indians around. Looks like a huntin' party but they could be mean. This is bad country for trackin', Coco. Too uneven, too much water. Then if they do turn off, it could be into the desert."

"I got no use for no desert."

"Farnum would chance it. He's got supplies."

"But what about the Injuns?"

"That's somethin' we'll have to look out for tomorrow."

"Huntin' parties don't look for trouble, do they?"

Buchanan said, "Accordin' to how they feel."

"There's plenty small game around, seems like."

"Apaches like women," said Buchanan.

"Peaceful Apaches don't try to grab no women," Coco said.

"Not unless there's a reason. Since Geronimo stirred 'em up there's no tellin' what they'll do."

"They know you. They know you're straight with 'em."

"They don't know I'm around," Buchanan said. "How's the bacon comin'?"

"I made a double ration. I knowed you'd be hungry tonight. Whenever we ain't gettin' nowhere, you're hungrier than usual. Which is hungry enough."

Buchanan sat on a rock. The horses were nibbling grass which had been fodder for the fugitives. One day—maybe less than a day—Farnum had managed to keep that distance between them. If he was heading for some place near Tucson there were many days ahead.

Coco said, "You mind that time we was chasin' deer up north?"

"Which time?"

"The time we didn't find any."

"I mind it."

"This is the way it was. And we finally trapped the bear. Montana, that was. He was some bear."

"It was Colorado. And I wouldn't say we trapped the bear. More like he trapped us." Buchanan felt for a scar on his rib cage where the grizzly had swiped him.

"We got him, though."

"Farnum's a bear. Conrad's a fox." Buchanan arose from the saddle and went to where the horses grazed.

He peered into the brush, walked around the perimeter of the fire and into the shadows beyond. He could see Amsy Burke's dead, broken face. He could see the smiling Mary Jane Brown, so neat and clean, serving them in the restaurant. He could see so many pictures of the recent past. He again touched the place where the bear had clawed him before he got in his last shot, into the ear. Coco, strong as he was, had had trouble getting the big carcass off of him. He had bled a lot that time.

And Farnum, like the grizzly, would die hard, knowing his fate if he were caught. The girl would die also unless a miracle took place; Buchanan faced that tragedy. No man could be more desperate than an escaped convict. He had felt the closing-in of the walls, sensed the desperation of the confined person in just the few hours before he had been freed from the miserable cell in Yuma prison. He knew what went on in the head of Farnum.

As to Conrad, Buchanan was not so certain. The slender man had seemed so inoffensive, so normal that there was no way to gauge his inner image. How did he see himself? Not as a sycophant to Farnum, Buchanan thought, he was too clever, too inventive to be a mere follower. He might accept a leader but inside him he was the clever one, the mover of events. Without Conrad's services, Farnum would still be in jail, and Amsy Burke would be alive, and Mary Jane still waiting on tables.

He came back to where Coco had coffee and cold food ready. He squatted on his heels cowboy-fashion, eating without relish.

Coco said, "'Member when we fought that fella out in San Francisco Bay? That was a time."

"I remember." But Buchanan's mind was far away, trying to evaluate the danger of the Indians and the fate of Mary Jane Brown. He listened and filled in with an occasional word as Coco rambled on. The sensitive black fighter was trying to help, to pull Buchanan out of a doldrum, and he knew he was not succeeding. In a little while they doused the fire and Buchanan took the first watch.

Coco slept like a baby. Buchanan walked the perimeter of the camp, his mind boiling. He did not sleep well.

In the morning he made one more wide cast around the camp. Under a tree he saw tracks. He followed them. They were made by moccasins which did not seem to be those of the Apache. His fears mounted. He almost stumbled over a broken arrow.

He bore it back to where Coco had the horses ready. He said, "You see this?"

"A busted arrow."

"And it ain't Apache. It's Yaqui."

"Yaqui? They belong down in Mexico."

"The Apaches raid them. They raid the Apache—or anybody gets in their path. They're worse than Apaches when on the warpath or on a raid like this bunch."

"Lordy me," said Coco. "Now we got a bear, a fox and a heap of bad Indians. How many of them you reckon?"

"Enough of 'em. They passed us. This arrow, it's from one of their mountain tribes. They won't have many guns, those people. They don't need 'em." He touched the feathered end. "They've been known to use poison on the flints."

"And they gone ahead? They between us and Farnum?"

"If they don't get turned off by somethin'."

"We best be on our way."

"And careful. Real careful."

He wondered if Farnum knew the difference between the volatile, but sometimes friendly, Apache, and the Yaqui. If not there might be an end to the chase very soon. And the girl would wind up in the mountains of Mexico. The Yaquis were fond of women slaves.

6

TIME became a blur to the girl. Slowly she realized she was becoming saddle-broken, so that the agony was less. But the lack of sleep, the journey up a long trail to the Mohawk Mountains, was soul-wracking.

They could not sleep enough to gain the required rest for her. Farnum backtracked every night. The watches became shorter, they traveled after dark.

Resting at last on a wide ledge of the mountain range, Farnum nursed his rifle and said, "At least they're driving us in the right direction."

"They're drivin' me loco," said Conrad. He looked at Mary Jane. "I don't know if she can make it."

"She'll make it. Them Indians would be worse company than us," Farnum said loud enough for her to overhear.

"One thing. They're between us and

whoever's on our trail. If anyone is on our trail."

"Buchanan," said Farnum. "You can depend on him."

"But how the hell we goin' to shake the damn Injuns?"

"Sooner or later they'll either get tired or they'll attack."

"It's a wonder they didn't catch up by now."

"Poor mounts. And we take care of our horses."

"Exceptin' we lost the pack animal."

Mary Jane shuddered. They had unpacked the sturdy little pony and shot him. They did not want the Indians to have him, she knew, but it had seemed cruel. Now they each carried what supplies they could save. Not enough for the ride ahead, she had gathered from their conversation. It was all a muddle, she did not know where they were going nor how long it would take. At times she did not know whether she was on the horse or trying to snatch some sleep. She was almost in complete despair . . . almost.

What they did not know was that Farnum's constant mention of Buchanan kept up her spirits. She thought of the big man and his strength and prayed.

Farnum said, "This country is rugged. Indians sometimes just don't want to bother, special the Apaches. They don't have any reason to follow us, not a good blood reason. I'm hopin' they'll just plain quit and go about their business."

Conrad jerked a thumb toward Mary Jane and whispered something. She could guess what it was. Apaches took women and traded them over the border. She knew all about that. But she also knew that Farnum believed he needed her. Once again her mind tumbled in a circle. What had her father often said? "Damned if you do and damned if you don't." That was about it. She saw no relief no matter how she twisted her thinking. She tried to sleep.

The first arrow came whizzing into the campfire at dawn. Conrad was on watch. He called to them. They came awake like wild animals, Farnum with rifle ready.

The small mesa on which they had encamped was shrouded in a mist. They could not see the enemy.

The head of the arrow nestled in the cool embers of the campfire. Farnum ordered, "Down. Flat. Don't fire."

Conrad, prone, asked, "You think we can parley with 'em?"

"I think we got to. There's plenty of 'em."

"Can't we mount up and try to ride through?"

"There's a breeze comin' up. They been on our trail for a couple days. What chance we got?"

"I can talk a little 'Pache."

"Wait and see if they want to talk."

"Why in hell should they, so many of 'em?"

"We still got guns. They like to live just as we do." They sounded as calm as if they were deciding what to have for breakfast. Mary Jane rolled out of her blankets, her teeth chattering.

"Can—can I have a gun, please?"

"Whatever for?" asked Farnum.

"To—to shoot myself, if—if I have to."

Conrad said, "She's got a right. She shoots us, it's all over for her. Why not?"

Farnum said, "Okay." He slid a sixshooter to where she could reach it. "But don't fire it unless I give you the word, you understand? There might be some way out if we don't kill one of 'em."

"I—I understand." She nursed the cold metal of the revolver as the sun increased its volume and the wind blew at the rolling clouds of silvery mist. There were no further arrows and no sound. It was frightening, uncanny, the waiting. She had heard of the patience of the Indian when he was on the warpath and in the mood. Now she wondered at it. Her mouth was dry and she trembled in every core of her body and limbs. She doubted she could fire the pistol accurately if the occasion demanded.

Farnum said, "Might's well stand up. They like to see you on the ground."

They arose. Mary Jane's knees shook until she made a tremendous effort. Then suddenly she was calm. Five bullets in the gun, she thought, one chamber under the hammer empty. She would shoot four times, then kill herself.

The breeze changed to a warm wind and the mist blew away. The Indians were aboard the ponies, a ring of them encircling the camp. Two of them immediately secured the horses of their captives.

Farnum said, "By God, Yaquis."

"Is that bad?" muttered Conrad.

"I spent four years in jail with a bad one." Farnum raised his right hand and said, *"Hola."*

The chief was immediately identifiable. He carried an ancient rifle. The others were armed with lances and bows and arrows. They were nearly naked, and taller than the Apaches, a sinewy race.

The chief said, *"Hola*. You are prisoners."

"Yes," said Farnum. He showed his rifle. "Unless many of us wish to die."

"It is better to live," responded the chief.

"We will speak then."

"No time for speaking. We take your guns, horses, squaw. You live."

"Without guns and horses we cannot live," said Farnum.

The chief rode close to Mary Jane, looked down upon her. His black eyes bored through her. She felt naked under his sweeping gaze.

He said, "Young. Strong. We will take her."

"Not the guns? Not the horses?"

"We will take them too. When we return."

It seemed hopeless. They could, Farnum knew. Trail along and pick them off one at a time. They could come any time of the night or day.

Cole Conrad had not spoken. Now he stepped forward. In his hand were three little red balls. He began to manipulate them. They rolled around his fingers, vanished, reappeared. The chief backed his horse suddenly, almost sending him down on his rump.

Farnum said, "My brother is a medicine man."

The Indians all watched Conrad's hands now. The balls vanished. There was a silk handkerchief, white in the ascending sun. He drew it slowly through his fingers. It changed colors, to red, to blue, to green. Then it too was gone.

Farnum said, "The pack."

He stepped forward and spoke to the chief. "We wish you no harm. But we cannot allow you to take everything from us. As has been said, it is better all should live."

They were watching him and his rifle. Conrad's clever hands busied themselves with his pack. He came out to them again solemn-faced, still without speaking. He lit a taper, held it before him, blew gently.

Fire spurted from his mouth in a long, thin stream. The Indians, even the chieftain, started back. Fire was sacred. To them it spelled life and death.

Farnum said, "We do not wish to destroy you. But beware."

Mary Jane had no idea what Farnum and the chief were saying to one another. She was amazed at Conrad's tricks. She managed only with effort to keep her jaw from going slack.

Farnum said, "One last display for your benefit. Then you must go and never return."

Misdirection worked this time. Their heads swiveled just a fraction of a second, to attend the words of the speaker. It was enough time for Conrad to extract a stick of dynamite wrapped in bright red, to ignite the fuse and send stick and cap flying skyward.

When it exploded the sound rolled in the damp aftermath of the mist like thunder. Conrad threw his arms wide and strings of multi-colored paper unrolled, fluttered—and burst into flame.

The Yaquis in the back ranks were already in motion. The chief lingered a moment, half-raised his rifle.

Conrad pointed a dramatic finger at him. Again fire seemed to spurt from his mouth.

The chief turned and ran. In a moment the Indians were gone.

Conrad spat and spat again. "That damn coal oil tastes like hell."

Farnum said, "Lordy, you been doin' that fire-spoutin' trick since you was ten."

"Good thing I carried some in case of need," said Conrad. "You never know when a fire's needed."

"We better get goin' fast," said Farnum. He looked at Mary Jane. "You able to move?"

"Just about," she told him. The reaction had set in. She listlessly allowed him to take the gun from her. She might have shot both of them, she thought, if she had been able to keep her nerves under control.

Farnum said, "If you'd tried to shoot us I was ready. It wouldn't be a nice thing for you to do after Cole saved us."

"No, it wouldn't," she said. "Thank you, Cole, for being so clever."

"It's what I do best." He made a mock bow. "Or nearly so."

She turned away from him to catch up the startled horses. Had they not been hobbled they would have been long gone, she knew. Farnum thought of everything. Conrad seemed able to squirm out of anything. They had her, there was no doubt in her mind. They were clever, dangerous men, and now she wondered if even Buchanan could catch up with them and handle them.

Buchanan said, "Indians ahead." He came down from the tree from whence he had been watching with his old field glasses. Coco was already mounted. They rode for the nearby high country. They went up over shale, the hoofs of the horses slipping and sliding. The Indians pursued.

They came to a hilltop. Buchanan reined in. Again he peered through the glasses. "We're losin' the trail of Farnum. Best to make a stand."

Coco said, "I ain't shootin' no guns at no Indians. They ain't done nothin' to me —yet."

"You run around and lay for 'em," suggested Buchanan. "Maybe you can get 'em to fight Queensbury rules."

Coco said, "It ain't no time for jokin'."

Buchanan unlimbered the Remington he was carrying. His .44-caliber bullets fitted both revolver and long gun. He chose a rock and peered down the slope. They were the Yaquis, he recognized. They had been between Farnum and his pursuit. Now they had come back, which meant that somehow Farnum and Conrad and the girl had managed to elude them.

He laid his first shot low, tumbling a rider. He sent the next high. A brave in the rear of the attack screamed and fell. The chief, riding up front, bent low and came on, then circled away, out of rifle range. The band followed him. They sat in a circle around him as he brandished an old gun. It was then Buchanan knew they were bearing nothing but their primitive weapons.

"What they doin'?" asked Coco. He was absolutely unafraid, merely curious.

"Palaverin'," said Buchanan. "Either they're goin' to bury their dead or they're goin' to try us."

"They'd ride up that slope and you with the guns?"

Buchanan was reloading. "The Yaqui ain't like the Apache. He'll try anything if he's feelin' it'll work."

It was hard to tell whether the chief was exhorting the braves or merely speaking with them. They moved hither and yon on their ponies, came to a halt. The chief held the old rifle under his right arm. The others brandished lances and bows.

Buchanan said, "Might be they're tryin' to scare us off this hill."

"Any time you're ready," said Coco. "The horses are rested."

The chief had ridden several yards in front of his braves. They had quieted down, sitting their ponies in a semi-circle. The chief walked his horse toward the hill. He reined in, sheathed his rifle, held up his right arm.

"He wants to parley," said Buchanan.

"You speak his language?"

"Never tried," said Buchanan. "Always could manage, though."

"Make him come up here," Coco begged. "You know I can't cover you case of trouble."

"He's got his rifle. I keep mine."

"I don't like it," Coco protested.

"Neither do I," Buchanan acknowledged. "Howsome ever."

He stuck his rifle in the boot and rode down hill. The chief awaited him, the Yaqui band held ranks. When the two came together there was, for a moment, no sound except the breeze rustling the brush. At once Buchanan knew the Yaqui chieftain was perturbed.

Buchanan asked, *"Habla español?"*

The chief nodded, shrugged. He made signs that were recognizable, signs that had enabled white man and Indian to communicate since the opening of the West.

Speaking slowly in Spanish, Buchanan said, "We have no quarrel with the Yaqui. We hunt for bad men—and a squaw."

"Aieee! The medicine man."

"Medicine man?"

"He put a curse upon us with fire. See, today we have already lost two braves to you."

"Fire, eh?" That would be a Conrad trick, Buchanan thought at once.

The chief made swift motions with lean, brown hands. He extended his cheeks and blew, waving. Buchanan looked at him closely. The chief was sweating.

"You do not fear this man?" the chief asked.

"There was a squaw with them?"

"Young squaw."

"Did you trail them?"

The chief vigorously shook his head. "Bad medicine!"

"Plenty bad medicine." It was an opportunity to be seized. Buchanan looked around, again made the peace sign. There was a small tree nearby. Dangling from it was a broken twig. Buchanan reached for his belt buckle. The little pistol always concealed therein was invisible in his huge hand. He fired, slid the Derringer from view, all in one swift motion. The twig fell to earth. The chief stared, swallowed hard.

Buchanan said, "We too have medicine. That was a bad man. The other man escaped from Yuma. You savvy Yuma Prison?"

The chief nodded vigorously. "So. Thus it is. You will destroy the bad medicine."

"That is my intention." He was not certain whether the Yaqui understood his words, but the meaning seemed to be clear. They stared hard at one another for a long moment. Then the chief wheeled his horse and rode back to his band. Buchanan did not turn his back upon them until they had filed southward and vanished from his view. Then he rode slowly back up the hill.

Coco said, "Coulda kilt you any second."

"They ran into Farnum," Buchanan said. "Conrad flummoxed them somehow. How about that? Prob'ly saved our lives, that clever little sneak."

"I don't give him no credit."

"Puts me more in mind of something I've been thinking on."

"Farnum's scary tough. But Conrad, he's scary smart."

133

"I'm thinking of the girl. If we get too close what'll happen to her?"

"We got to get close." Coco opened and closed his hands. "Close enough, when they don't expect it."

"That can't happen in open country. They know it. So we track 'em. But we keep our distance."

"Makes it twice as hard, don't it?"

"We knew it wasn't goin' to be easy."

They had fallen farther behind during the colloquy with the Indians. There was nothing to do but retrace their way and pick up trail. It was a task Buchanan had faced many times. It was a skill at which he excelled. Still, it was a tedious proceeding, and he knew it would take every bit of his experience and conditioning. He studied the map he had obtained from the hotel clerk.

The trading post at Sentinel seemed the nearest settlement. It was about forty-seven miles from Walton on the road to Gila Bend. On the south were the Growler Mountains. The Aguila range was closer. It was purely a matter of conjecture which route Farnum would take. He would leave the banks of the Gila River, Buchanan believed, because that seemed the obvious way to go. There were men hunting him. He had to pick the least likely ways among river, mountains, and desert. The only possible way to trace him was to forge ahead, pick up his night camps and go on from there.

Again, thinking of the trickery of Conrad and the desperation of Farnum, he knew it would be perilous to be seen too close upon the heels of the fugitives.

He heaved a deep breath and said, "Nothin' to do but our best. We just keep moseyin' along."

"Better than bein' shot at by Injuns," said Coco. "Reckon we better eat?"

"Later," said Buchanan.

Surprised but willing, Coco mounted the roan horse and followed over the hill en route to wherever Farnum, Conrad, and the girl had last encamped.

7

IN Yuma, Sheriff Jake Lee brought in two disconsolate escapees and delivered them over to the prison. Warden Browning was grateful but preoccupied: his job was endangered, and he was busy pulling political strings. Lee went disgustedly down to the restaurant run by Hotchkiss and ordered an enormous meal. The owner came and sat with him.

"Any news from Farnum?"

"All kinds of news," said the sheriff moodily. "He's been here, he's been there. The Rangers have almost grabbed him a couple times—they say. Bounty-hunters brought in a half-dozen people who ain't Farnum nor Conrad."

"Mary Jane?"

"She's been seen with 'em. They're keepin' her alive, all right. No doubt about that."

"No idea where they're headin'?"

"If they knew the Rangers would be waitin' for 'em."

"That pore little old gal."

"She's got one chance," the sheriff said.

"Buchanan?"

"Ain't nobody heard a word from Buchanan and Coco Bean."

"You don't think Farnum coulda bush-whacked 'em?"

"He could've. But it figures somebody would've found the bodies. They been on the run for almost a month now. They been dodgin' around until nobody can figure which way they're headed. They been doublin' back and stealin' here and beggin' there, always polite, always in that mealy-mouth way Farnum has got. What with him palaverin' and Conrad doin' tricks, it seems they got everybody confabulated."

"Of the whole gang that escaped, how many got clean away?"

"Just them. The dummies mainly made for Mexico or California. Those that went t'other way, the Rangers picked up. But

Farnum, he smells danger. He's plumb smart like a fox."

"A month's a heap of time to stay loose with the whole territory lookin' for you."

Lee said, "A month's a long time to have Buchanan on your tail."

"Buchanan never was a lawman, was he?"

Lee chuckled. "Not if he could help it. He got trapped a couple times into wearin' a badge, but it didn't take. No, Buchanan's a free soul. But I'll tell you somethin.'"

"Yeah?"

"I'd rather have a whole Apache nation on my heels than have Buchanan interested in me."

Hotchkiss fretted. "There's Injuns out. Apaches, Yaquis. Farnum must've run across them. Buchanan, too."

"Buchanan knows Apaches. The Yaquis, they're different, but Buchanan and the Indians always seem to work things out." Lee shook his head. "No. It comes down to Farnum and Conrad against Buchanan and Coco Bean."

"The difference bein' the gal."

"The gal," agreed Hotchkiss. "The good Lord protect her."

The new girl brought the food. Somehow it didn't taste the same as it had when Mary Jane was serving, but Jake was hungry from his long trip. He fell to as the pair sat silently at the table, thinking of Buchanan and Coco and wondering.

Farnum pulled at his belt buckle. The girl was, he knew, close to sheer exhaustion. He had seen to it that she had the last of the food, despite Conrad's unspoken opposition. Farnum was still worried about Conrad and Mary Jane. His cousin had turned in upon himself during the weeks of running and hiding. Cole was a different person when his tricks were not of daily use.

They had made it, somehow, down to the Tucson Mountains. There was little more territory to cover, but Farnum could detect danger from every point. He felt secure in the high place, but it was necessary to have food. They had been eating small game, and it was not enough to sustain them. The girl looked poorly, he thought. He could not afford to have her collapse.

And Buchanan, with the black man in attendance, was still on the trail. Perhaps not close—but there, somewhere. Farnum had backtracked enough times to be aware of this. There was no shaking the big man. It would have to come to a showdown sooner or later. He was determined to choose the place.

He was not afraid of Buchanan. He was a bit fearful of his cousin's preoccupation with the girl. On the other hand, he knew Cole's attitude toward money. There was fifty thousand at stake, half of which Cole had pledged. He wondered if Cole would get it into his head that the girl plus all the money might well be his. Trickery— it had always been Cole's way since they were children.

He knew a few tricks of his own, he told himself. He led them over a hill and down an arroyo. To his surprise there lay ahead of them a small, well-built cattle spread.

He paused, hand upraised. It was noontime, and smoke came from a chimney. There was no sign of life, no cowboys, only a tiny corral and few head of beef in a pasture, a garden, and a grove of fruit trees.

He then saw the stream trickling down, giving life to this oasis in otherwise vacant land. A man with vision, with courage, he sighed. There was a washline and hung upon it were small pieces of clothing that could only be those of a child. A man, a woman and at least one child, here in a semiwilderness, had put down roots.

Cole said, "Grub."

"The way we do this, we go in quietlike," Farnum told them. "Mary Jane, you're our sister. We've been lost and are only now getting straightened out. There's a good lookout on top of the barn. We'll make excuses to sashay up there now and then."

"Why all this?" demanded Cole. "What are they, lawmen? We go in and take what we want."

"A couple weeks ago you wouldn't have

talked like that," Farnum told him. "You're gettin' nervish, Cole. You play this my way, you understand?"

Cole said, "Why can't Mary Jane be my wife instead of my sister? It could work out nice that way."

Farnum bestowed upon him a long, contemplative stare. Then he said, "I hope you're jokin'. I hope you're gettin' back your senses, Cole. I truly do."

"Sure, I'm funnin'," Cole said. "Let's go down and get somethin' in our bellies. I'm pure starvin' for some home cookin'."

They rode very slowly toward the ranch. A man stepped out of the barn, lean, in his forties perhaps. In his hands was a formidable shotgun. From the rear door of the house a woman appeared with a rifle leveled. Farnum threw up his empty hands.

"We mean no harm. We're kinda lost, me and my brother and sister. Headin' Tucson way."

"You're off the trail." The man had a resonant voice. His eyes were blue and sharp.

Farnum said ruefully, "Tried a short

cut. Some jasper gave us a bum steer. We have money to pay for food and shelter."

The man relaxed. "My name's Grover. That's my wife Adah. Sorry to seem to be ready for war, but there's been Indians and rustlers around. We don't get no outside news very often."

"We're the Jackson family," said Farnum. "Cole, here and Mary Jane."

Grover looked toward the house. His wife came forward, trailing the rifle. She was a plain, sturdy woman, straight-shouldered. "Names don't mean much out here, do they?" she asked briskly. "If you got hard cash, we sure can use it, not meaning to be inhospitable. Little Johnny needs things I purely can't make for him, so does Mr. Grover. Put up your horses and come on in. Dinner's about ready, always extries."

The barn was well kept. There was feed, hay and straw for the horses. Farnum's quick eyes missed nothing. Grover was a man who knew his business. They did not unpack what was left of their belongings. They went straight for the house. Mary

Jane staggered once, and Cole caught her elbow. He seemed reluctant to release it and she pulled away from him. Farnum scowled as they entered the rear door into the kitchen.

The boy was about eight, too young to be much use excepting for garden chores. He was delighted to see company. He hid shyly at first behind his mother's apron, then sidled up to Mary Jane and began a conversation asking about her trip and where she was going and how did she like riding a horse across country. Farnum filled in the answers when Mary Jane hesitated.

There was a pot of soup on the wood stove. Mrs. Grover cut slices of meat from a roast. Potatoes were already boiling and there were ripe, red tomatoes from the garden. She cut thick hunks from home-made bread and planted a dish of butter in the center of the large table. Then, arms akimbo, she looked straight at Farnum.

"Excuse me, but you did say cash."

"Now, Adah," said her husband.

"Oh, there's been times when we could

144

afford handouts," she replied fiercely. "We gladly give 'em. But now it's need. We get to town once a month. There's so much we have to get and so little money. You people understand that."

Farnum said with utmost politeness, "We certainly do, Miz Grover. Give her money, Cole, give her enough."

The clever hands produced a coin and laid it upon the table. Mrs. Grover stared at it. "Twenty dollars. That's too much."

"We can afford it," Farnum assured her. "Buy somethin' pretty, somethin' you don't really need. It's always a satisfaction to be extravagant."

Grover said, "Well, what with the fodder and all—" He pocketed the gold piece. Farnum sensed the relief in the man. It was always the same with these hard-working folks who lived off the land. They were always short of cash. Barter was their way of life. He could never cut it himself, he knew, not without a twinge of regret. And Cole saw money only as a means to gamble for more money, to hornswoggle a way to high living. In the past five and a half years, Farnum had often wondered why, but had never come up with a conclusion. He still did not know exactly what he was going to do with twenty-five thousand dollars—if he could keep Cole from getting it away from him.

They sat down at the table. All ate with gusto, excepting Mary Jane. She seemed not to taste the food she dutifully put into her mouth. She was eating only for the strength to keep going, Farnum thought. He felt guilty about the girl, but he knew she was their only salvation if Buchanan caught up with them.

It might well be that he would have to kill Buchanan. In that case, the girl would become a real problem. She would have to be sequestered in a safe place until such time as they could get clear of the country. It was a situation which gnawed at his mind during the long night watches.

Grover was saying, "If we only had a good seed bull. Old Sam is gettin' down at the hindquarters. I could clear some more land for grazin' and in a couple years make a bunch to take up the trail, 'stead of sellin' in Tucson at low prices."

"Right," said Farnum, pushing back his chair, replete with the solid food.

"There's pie," said Mrs. Grover.

"Later, maybe." He took his rifle from the corner, trying to be unobtrusive, knowing he was observed. He went out to the barn and climbed into the loft. There was, as usual, an escape hatch to the roof. He sat for a moment, allowing his digestive apparatus to work. He looked to the far horizon westward. If anyone was coming it would be in that direction, down through the arroyo. It had been a long haul, the longest of his career. The hard life of the prison had prepared him for it, but he knew that the girl was near the end of her string and that Cole was wearing thin. There was not much more distance to travel, as only he was aware, but it would be difficult and dangerous. He would need Cole at the end. He had to keep his cousin in line, make him ready.

He was turning ways and means over in his mind when he saw the two horsemen.

He raised the rifle and waited. It was Buchanan, all right. He could not mistake the big man on the black horse, with his equally burly companion. He estimated the range. Now Farnum was cold, every instinct trained upon the task. He had to choose the exact moment, he had no illusions about what would happen if he missed. There was no time to call for Cole and the girl. He dared not move a muscle lest Buchanan espy him prone upon the roof.

They stopped. He saw Buchanan dismount and examine the earth. The trail of three horses was plain enough at the place where they had come to soft soil. He held his breath.

Buchanan stood erect. He put out a warning hand to Coco. Farnum elevated his sight. It would be his only opportunity for a straight-on shot. He fired.

Buchanan went down. Coco leaped to earth and sent the horses bolting for cover. They knew their business, those two, Farnum thought, scrambling for the hay-mow, the ladder leading down. Cole was already running from the house, dragging the girl. The Grovers, nonplussed for the moment, gathered in the doorway unarmed.

Farnum led out the horses, fed but not rested enough. There was none of Grover's stock at hand worth seizing. He yelled one word, "Buchanan!"

A bullet whizzed past his ear.

He stopped dead in his tracks. Cole whipped out a knife and seized Mary Jane, drew her close, applied the blade to her throat.

Buchanan was on his knees, his rifle somehow in his hands. Coco knelt at his side. Farnum could see no blood, but he knew he had hit the big man.

It was Coco who walked toward them. Farnum could have picked him off, but it was neither the time nor place. When they were within speaking distance, Coco called out, "Let the gal go and we'll give you a start."

"Come any closer and the girl is dead," said Farnum.

"Then you'll be dead, too," Coco told him.

"And what good would that do? Nobody knows where the plunder is hidden. Me and Cole, we'll be buried with the girl. It don't make sense no ways."

Coco hesitated. This was more in Buchanan's line, but he had been told to parley and parley he would. Maybe Buchanan could get a bead on Cole and drop him before he could harm the girl.

Farnum was saying to the Grovers, "Those are bad men. They are trying to steal our money."

The family hesitated.

Coco said, "We ain't interested in the money. Only the girl."

This was bad, Farnum thought. This could turn the thoughts of the Grovers around; the Grovers had weapons and seemed quite ready to use them.

He said, "You and your thievin' friend just keep your distance. We're ridin' out right now. You follow and the girl gets it."

He motioned to the horses. He mounted, shielding Cole. The girl had no choice but to crawl aboard her pony. Cole, nimble always, drew a revolver, staying close to her. Coco watched them, helpless. They rode out, going quickly around the house.

Mrs. Grover said puzzledly, "They were threatenin' their sister."

Grover went for his gun. Coco ran down the slope to the house. There was no sight of the fugitives by the time Grover reappeared.

Coco said, "That was Farnum and his cousin and a gal they kidnapped. I got a wounded man up yonder. How you folks feel about that?"

"Farnum? Rube Farnum? That nice man?" demanded Mrs. Grover.

"The same nice man that killed a few people on his way," Coco told them.

He turned his back and went up the slope to where Buchanan, on one knee, was trying to maintain consciousness. The bullet had struck him in the shoulder. He was quite sure it had gone through, having had much experience with bullet wounds, but he felt dizzy. Worse, he felt completely frustrated. Farnum had been in his sights and he had been able to do absolutely nothing about it. There had been over a month of hard chase. The trail had twisted and turned, always proceeding southwest in the end, but never constant. It had been the meanest, toughest chase of his many, and now he was bleeding and the fugitives were again gone. He waited grimly for Coco to come and get him.

Buchanan asked the boy and Mrs. Grover to leave the kitchen. He heated a poker. Coco ran a clean sliver of cloth through the flesh of his left shoulder. He had been correct. The bone had not been more than nicked. With Grover's aid, the wound was cauterized. The herbal lotion, provided them long ago by an Indian girl of the Crow Nation, was then applied. Buchanan ached, he was hungry and angry and mortified, but he was able to eat what was left of the Grover fodder.

The story was soon told. Mrs. Grover shook her head.

"A nicer, more polite man I never met.

His Cousin—Conrad?—gave us a twenty-dollar piece. Was that stolen?"

Buchanan said, "If Conrad had it, you can bet it was not gained honestly. Only thing is, he might have swindled a crook. So keep it in good health, Miz Grover. We will pay for whatever we use here. Just thank your stars that you nor yours were hurt."

"Such a nice, polite man," she repeated.

"He has that way about him," said Coco. "Also he shot Tom without warning, in cold blood. And he'd do the same to anybody stood in his way."

"That's the way it is with Farnum," agreed Buchanan.

"But for the grace of God," muttered Grover, then stopped, looking at his wife, his son. "Well, I seen good boys swing a wide loop and hang for it. May have branded a maverick or two my own self when I was gettin' started. Manners don't make the man, Adah."

"Jonathan!"

He grinned. "Buchanan understands."

Buchanan nodded. "I've seen it all.

Believe me, lady, this country brings out the inside of a man. Your husband's a worker and he's honest. A blind person could see that. If you'll be as good as to let us use your barn, we'll rest up for the rest of the chase."

"I hope you don't smoke," she said, bringing a lantern.

"Neither of us ever did get the habit," Buchanan assured her.

He went to the barn. Coco arranged a bed of straw. Buchanan lay upon it and stared at the roof. "If I'd only come in more cautious. If I'd only realized we were so close to 'em. I never thought they'd stop at a place like this."

Coco said, "If the dog hadn't stopped to do you know what, he'd of caught the rabbit. Now you get some sleep and let that Injun medicine do its work, and we'll be able to git on with it."

It was not only good advice. It was the only advice possible under the circumstances. Buchanan closed his eyes and gently cursed himself for a fool.

In the morning his shoulder was stiff

and sore. Mrs. Grover had a hearty breakfast ready, for which she refused payment.

"Let's say those bad people paid for it," she told them. "You can rest up here long as you want."

"Thank you, ma'am," said Buchanan. "We'll ride along. Farnum was out of supplies. What's the nearest town?"

"It's scarcely a town," said her husband. "Called Sentinel."

"They'll be in and out of there by now. Maybe we can pick up their next move, though. We do thank you."

"We were lucky," Grover said soberly. "Farnum might have killed us all."

Buchanan shook his head. "Not his style." He tousled the head of little Johnny with his right hand. "People is strange sometimes, sonny. Always remember Farnum."

They mounted and rode toward Sentinel.

The Grover family watched them go. Then they moved toward the house. Johnny went about his chores, as man and wife stood together at the rear door.

"Adah," he said, "keep the shotgun ready."

"My lands, you don't expect more trouble?"

"It comes in threes," he told her. "Further and more, when there's criminals loose more'n a couple people will be after them."

"You reckon they'll come by here?"

"Keep the gun handy."

He stayed near the barn, making small chores. Thus he saw four men come to the arroyo as had the previous invaders of his peaceful layout. He took down a six-gun belt and strapped it on. He picked up his rifle and called to his wife. He could see the barrel of the shotgun at the window. He turned and waited.

The man who led the quartet rode in. He wore a badge on his loose vest. He was unshaven and had the appearance of a hard case. The other three remained behind him, fanning out when they saw that Grover was armed.

The leader said, "I'm Marshal Cassidy We're looking for an escaped prisoner and

156

his friend. You seen anyone like o' that lately?"

"Maybe. Maybe not," said Grover.

"You seen a big man on a black horse with a nigger along with him?"

"Maybe. Maybe not."

"There's four of us, my friend. We want answers."

Grover said, "There's a few of us. Take a look at the window. Don't move. Just look."

Cassidy squinted. He nodded. "Okay. You got us covered. Now tell me, you for the law or agin it?"

"You ain't the local lawman," Grover told him. "Odds are that you're bounty-huntin'. So get along."

Cassidy nodded. "They been here. Seen some spots up yonder looked like blood. Seen enough tracks to tell me lots I want to know. We don't mean no harm to decent folks. We'll go."

"I'll be watchin'," Grover told him.

"I bet you will. Man out here with a spread like this." Cassidy lifted a hand. The others rode around the corner of the house. The shotgun barrel vanished, but it would reappear at another convenient window, he figured. "Okay, mister. We'll just folley train. Sooner or later. . . . Sooner or later."

"So's you don't hang around here," said Grover harshly.

"Wouldn't be healthy." Cassidy gave him a crooked grin and followed his men.

It was many hours before Grover felt that he could do some tracking of his own. Marshal Cassidy had picked up the trail of Buchanan and Coco Bean, he found. He went back home, still uneasy but feeling that he could defend his castle, such as it was.

A mile along the trail the man called Snade rode up alongside Cassidy. He had a scar on his lip, which made him lisp. "You didn't try that federal-marshal line on that jasper back yonder?"

"Snade, there's men you try to fool. And there's men you walk around. That man had us under guns. Best to walk around and not waste time nor powder and shot."

"You figure Buchanan's hurt?"

"I dunno who's hurt. But whichever, it's an ace in the hole for us."

"I got to give you credit. You said get horses, and then follow Buchanan."

"I know all about Buchanan," Cassidy said. His face turned sour. His eyes glowed. "You seen him. He's plain, point-blank dynamite. There's only one way to git him."

"And you know it?"

"I know enough to follow along. Play his game, there ain't no better."

"And then?"

"Then comes the time."

"Morgan, Gonzales and me, there ain't no man can stand against us. But supposin' Buchanan ketches up with Farnum—and they throw in together?"

"If that happens there ain't nothin' to do but fight."

Snade persisted, "Is it worth it?"

"The bounty money, no. The fifty thousand loot, what do you think?"

Snade said, "Any way we can get both?"

Cassidy regarded him. "I always knew

you was smart. You think about that. Don't talk about it to Morgan and Gonzales. Think hard about it."

"I'll do that."

"And Snade?"

"Yeah?"

"Don't think about gettin' more than your share."

The twisted lip curled. "I ain't that smart. Nor that dumb, neither."

"Just remember whose notion this was, who brought you this far—and try and figure what to do when we close in on them. Because there ain't no way they can cover from the four of us."

"Specially Gonzales."

"That's keerect. Specially Gonzales. Give him some more tequila and let him smell out the trail."

"Cassidy?"

"Yeah?"

"Gonzales, he wouldn't know what to do with all that money."

"Neither would Morgan, but Morgan's a real fast gun."

Snade was satisfied. "I'm a faster gun than Morgan."

"It'll work out," said Cassidy. "It'll work out real fine. But the best way would be if we all closed in on Farnum at the same time. That would be prime. Buchanan on our side."

"I'll think on that, too."

"There's one thing: Every man's got his price."

"Not Buchanan."

"Oh, yes, he has."

"Nobody can buy Buchanan. What price you gonna give?"

"The gal, Snade," said Cassidy. "Think on the gal."

They rode on the plain trail which Buchanan had made no effort to cover.

Morgan, a slim youth, was chinless. His eyes seldom blinked, his hands were slim, gloved, he sat his horse with great grace. Gonzales was thick-bodied and wore a gigantic mustache. His brown face was expressionless; he seemed half-asleep. He took the lead whenever there was doubt about the tracks they were following, fell back uninterested when the way was clear. Every so often he sucked on a brown bottle. They rode without haste, content to bring up in the rear of the chase.

Cassidy had been around a long time, under different names and guises. He was a man of various facets. He felt neither proud nor diminished by any one of them. He had worked all sides of the law in every territory of the West. Originally from the east, he had grown up in Texas, followed the cattle drives, found hard work unsatisfactory, trotted the owl hoot trail without much luck and turned to fast-gun, itinerant law business. He was smart enough and tough enough to clean up a few of the early cowtowns without allowing anyone to learn of his devious ways. He had been on top for a while, lost his position because of greed, and come down, temporarily, to Walton.

Now he was on the prowl again. He had learned to pick his company, he believed. He had the three men he needed to attain this one last goal. He could handle them —and he felt that he always had an answer, always a way toward success. He was not a coward. He was a man who meant to get things his way sooner or later, and he was heartily merciless when it came to methods.

He said to Snade, "This is the biggest stake ever. You know that. So keep thinkin' and keep straight."

"If I wasn't thinkin' straight I wouldn't be here," said Snade. "It ain't no Sunday School picnic."

"It will be afore we're finished," said Cassidy.

The way was long but they proceeded at their leisure.

8

MARY JANE tightened her belt. They had been without food for two days. She had been losing weight all along, and now she was a wraith. And still the eyes of Cole Conrad were upon her.

She had tried in every way possible to secure a weapon, any kind of small defense for the time she felt was coming. They were too watchful, it had been impossible. She had not breathed fully and completely, she thought, since she had been abducted. She had no way of knowing if Buchanan was alive and on the trail. The others did not count.

They had encountered hundreds of enemies, bounty-hunters, Rangers, local officers. Each time, Farnum had managed by one means or another to avoid being caught, and was rarely seen. The man was amazing.

Now they were on the edge of desert. Farnum did not choose to be there. The manhunt had forced a detour. She gathered that much from their low-voiced conversation. It seemed that her ears had been sharpened by privation, or by her constant attempts at eavesdropping. They could not cross the desert without supplies. She had no idea where they were, did not know what lay beyond the stretch of sand and sage. She only knew she was starved, numbed with the fear. They were talking now, apart from her, between a copse of trees and the swamp which edged the desert.

Conrad said, "You got rid of Buchanan, but every other son is on the warpath."

"You got rid of the Indians and the white man took over," Farnum agreed. He seemed no different than when he had broken jail weeks ago. The fact that he was gaunt did not detract from his strength. "I'm going to take a look."

He was climbing the tallest tree available at the moment. She watched him, fascinated. Conrad moved close to her, smiled his significant smile.

"Rube'll get us through. Don't you fret, Mary Jane. We'll come out of this all right."

"That's what you think." His optimism was skin-deep. He put on a brave front when talking with her alone but she had detected the nervousness beneath the surface—as she knew had Farnum. Conrad was making an attempt at it, but he was not of the stuff of his cousin. She said, "You think because he shot Buchanan that he killed him? Buchanan don't die easy."

"Buchanan. He's the only one you think about. There's hundreds out there." He waved his hand, and produced the inter- changeable red balls. He juggled them a moment, his smile fixed. "Rube'll find a way."

The worst of it was that Farnum had so far always indeed found a way. He now shinned down from the tree. His expression had not changed. He said calmly, "They're on all three sides.

They're leaving the desert to us. They know we didn't steal enough supplies at the last stop."

"How about the horses?" asked Conrad.

"They can't make it nohow. They're fat on grass, but short on oats, and rest."

Conrad looked at Mary Jane. "We make them an offer?"

"Not yet."

"Why not?"

"The Rangers are that way. There's a bunch of people that way." Farnum gestured with his thumb. "There's a strung-out gang that look like they ain't organized back there."

"That's the way we came."

"We've never been headed direct to where we're going," Farnum answered him. "What was that story you told me about Buchanan down in Mexico after the prizefight?"

Conrad said, "That's a hell of a good way to get killed."

Farnum now in his turn looked at Mary Jane. "Maybe."

"You mean she rides in front?"

Farnum did not remove his gaze. It was odd how his face could harden in a split instant. He spoke softly. "You wouldn't try to get away, would you, Mary Jane? With me behind you?"

She shuddered. "No. I wouldn't want to die that way."

"Tighten up the cinches," Farnum said. "Let these nags know we mean business."

He went to the horse. The box marked with the double X was still among the few possessions that he had managed to save, she noted. He motioned to her. She tightened the cinch and climbed atop the horse. Conrad hesitated, then followed suit.

Farnum said, "They got our trail, but they haven't spotted us. So ride as quiet as possible until you see them. Then drive straight and shoot."

"Which way do we go if we get through?"

"South by east," said Farnum. "There's some open country and some coulees. I'll see that we don't ride into a blind canyon. I know this country."

"We're gettin' close and now this," muttered Conrad.

"Not all that close," Farnum said.

It was strange that Farnum had not trusted them with his true destination, Mary Jane thought. It was also, she believed, clever. She knew that Conrad had fixed upon getting her one way or another. She had been with them so long, day and night, that she could read them well. She confessed a sneaking, wry respect for Farnum although she feared him to her bones. Conrad was like an evil, small boy with an underlying foxiness. There was also a weakness revealed by his fixation upon her person. He was the more dangerous to her.

Farnum said to her, "Lie low, keep your head down. If you see anyone shooting your way use your horse for protection. Like the Indians, you know?"

"I know." She was not at all sure she could manage, but there was no alternative. Farnum was already riding, urging her horse to the forefront. She reached up and undid the bandanna that held her hair

169

tight to her head. Flowing locks might possibly prevent someone taking a shot at her. On the other hand, she had no delusions about mercy when bounty money was involved. She shivered once, then put heels to the horse.

It became a dreamlike ride. They were going at top speed when they came within range of the first rifleman. He lifted his gun, stared, fired. The bullet sped by her ears and she instinctively ducked. Behind her she heard Farnum cry, "To the left."

She neck-reined and the horse, frightened, veered. Farnum was shooting now and then Conrad. There were men in front of her. She drove straight at them, and they dropped to the ground and the shooting became general.

The horse was flying. She clung desperately to the reins. They were going down a slight grade, which increased the speed and also the danger of a horse slipping and falling. The ground was uneven but there were trees ahead. She went into them. Farnum and Conrad were still firing, not often, reserving their ammunition. She never knew how many were hit by their gunfire but she heard shouts and a scream.

She glanced behind her. Farnum waved to go ahead. He was cool, erect in the saddle, looking back. Conrad was a dozen yards from him. The lead still sang as the bounty-hunters continued to attack, but the song was now low-key and sporadic. She could scarcely believe that at least one of the horses had not been hit.

They were suddenly alone, and Farnum was abreast of her. He now led the way. They went down a steep hill into a small ravine and then labored up the other side.

Farnum said in his cool manner, "If we have not attracted the Rangers, there should be a way."

They followed him. He cut across and eastward, then south, then east again. The horses were tiring, but she felt that they had come through the line of attack and were on a definite course.

The desert was now behind them, parallel to them. Farnum led them to water and they dismounted. The horses had to be restrained from drinking too much from the clear stream.

Conrad said, "Cousin, you sure know your countryside."

"We had a bunch operated around here," Farnum said, then was silent for a moment before he spoke again. "Never did like trainin' with a crew."

"You and me. Loners, they call us."

Mary Jane bound up her hair and replaced the kerchief. Her stomach was empty and growling at her.

Farnum said, "There's a town about ten miles from here. We'll hit it at night."

"Long as there's grub," Conrad said.

"It's a little place. No big settlements where we're going," Farnum assured them. "We don't want to be seen now. When we get food we'll circle around behind them."

"And then?"

"Then we'll be where I want us to be," he said.

Mary Jane could read hope and assurance in him, as if the successful drive through the pursuers had inspired him.

Conrad said to her, "You sure did ride, Mary Jane. Never did see a lady so cool-like."

She refused to look at him. Farnum did not comment. They remounted and rode in the direction he had indicated. The dull, heavy fear returned to her innards.

The young doctor at Sentinel, en route to bigger and better surroundings, had said, "Mr. Buchanan, you are a most remarkable specimen. The wound is clean. You should be resting, but you seem fit enough."

Buchanan said, "Give credit to an Indian girl we met once some time ago. She provided the salve."

"I wish I had the prescription," said the doctor.

But now they were on the road, and for once in his life Buchanan weighed less than two hundred and forty pounds. Coco was accustomed to training on little food, and he fared better, but neither was in top condition. They rode toward the desert and reined in as one.

There was a group around a dead man. They were digging a grave. They seized their weapons.

Buchanan said, "Hold everything. We're on the same trail."

One of the men said, "Watch out if you find them. The gal rides with them."

"Just like she's one of 'em," said another. "Could be she's joined up. She sure led the charge."

"Charge?"

"They come straight at us. She was in the lead. She didn't try to roll off her hoss."

"She coulda taken a chance. Charley here, he fired over her head."

"Saw her hair flyin', knew it had to be the gal from Yuma," said the man addressed as Charlie. "I coulda got her."

"Then Farnum and the other, they laid down fire," said the first man. "Never seen nothin' like it. Right straight at us. Say, you're Buchanan, ain't you?"

"That's right."

"You got in his line o' fire?"

"I was lucky." He wore the arm in a light sling.

"You must be short of fodder."

"Plenty short. Since Sentinel, in fact."

"Well, light and share," said Charlie. "We got some cold vittles."

"Just let's put poor Jake down. Farnum got him point-blank."

"He the only one you lost?"

"Yeah. We're not lawmen, Mr. Buchanan. Just out lookin' to collect the reward, y'know?"

Charlie said, "And I, for one, had enough of it."

"Me too."

They went on with the burial of their late companion. Buchanan gratefully accepted meat and bread and cold beans. Coco shook his head, but helped with the lowering of the corpse into the earth.

Charlie asked, "You goin' to track on after 'em?"

"It's coming night," said Buchanan. "It always is when we get this close."

"Make camp with us?"

"Glad to."

He removed the sling. His arm was mending swiftly and he had something on his mind. He asked, "You see anything of a lawman named Cassidy and three others?"

Charlie said, "We seen 'em. They didn't appear to be followin' Farnum, though."

"Uh-huh," said Buchanan. He was right, then. Cassidy was depending upon him and Coco. He rested beside a fire as they produced a bottle and passed it around. They had a few things to say about Jake, the dead man. They were simple folk, he saw. They should be attending to their own business rather than chasing Farnum.

When night had fallen, there were a moon and some stars. Buchanan slept, then awakened. He had an alarm in his head which allowed him, under stress, to wake up at any time he chose. He walked Nightshade out of the camp and mounted and rode.

He traveled no more than five miles when he saw the flickering light of a fire. He walked far enough to make certain that he was correct. Cassidy and his men were trailing, all right. They were trailing Buchanan.

He thought about it on the way back to the encampment. Cassidy could be a terrible danger to Mary Jane Brown. He would not spare her; he had said as much back in Walton. He would shoot first and answer questions later. It amounted to another challenge. There would be a second showdown before this chase ended, that was for certain.

He lay down and thought deeply about it. He had a hunch again. He believed in his hunches. They had pulled him on strange errands many a time and almost always they had paid off. He went back to sleep, favoring his left shoulder.

At dawn it was Coco, with his broken-knuckled but gentle hands, dressing the wound, insisting on one more application of the salve. "We got to make us a trip back up north to get more of this," he was saying.

"You want to see the Indian girl again is what you mean."

"Nemmine that." Coco wrinkled his brow. "Figures she's married and got kids by now. Indian life ain't for me. Just let us get Mary Jane back and find us some fishin', and then find us a fight to make some money."

Buchanan winced as the pain fleetingly hit him. "You just had a fight."

"That hunk of nothin'? That wasn't a fight, that was a joke."

"It would've been a bad joke, wasn't for Conrad."

"People sure do funny things," Coco said. "Course he had his own money in there. Money to help them along when he got Farnum loose."

"They're a smart pair," Buchanan said. "So smart they got me thinkin' backwards and around the hill."

The camp was wakening. A fire was started. Charlie came to them.

"Everything okay?"

"If we could pay you for some food to get along on," suggested Buchanan.

"That'll be all right. We ain't none of us from far away." The man was somewhat

178

shamefaced. "Didn't have no right chasin' anybody like Farnum. Had to lose Jake to learn."

"Where are the Rangers?"

"Out to the southwest. Somebody said they figure Farnum hid his money around Tucson. Seems they agree."

"And there's bounty-hunters everywhere."

"Just about," said Charlie.

"And Farnum keeps himself, his cousin and the girl free as the air," said Coco.

Buchanan nodded. "He's smart, all right." He accepted coffee as Charlie went back to the fire to attend the breakfast. "These men are children compared to him."

"We ain't doin' much better."

"Worse," admitted Buchanan. "Exceptin' we're alive. You know, it figures Farnum was just as smart five and a half years ago as he is now."

"Could be. Though he did have thinkin' time."

"He stole the money. He killed the cashier. He got away for awhile. He had

179

fifty thousand dollars in hand. Yet when they caught him he didn't have the loot."

"That much everybody knows."

"And they think he hid it near Tucson."

"He got caught near Tucson, they said."

"But he had time. Now what would a real smart man do with that cash?"

"Hide it good. Which he did. You heard how many was lookin' for it."

"In caves. Diggin' holes in the ground. Lookin' for line camps, of which there are damn few hereabouts. No, he didn't bury the money. They'd have found it if he'd done that."

"He didn't swallow it."

"He put it in the safest place he could dream up."

"And where would that be?" demanded Coco.

"I don't know."

"But you got a hunch."

"I got a hunch."

"Like what?"

"Like the way he's been circlin' around, trying to break through here and there, he's headin' for the place. And it's the last anybody'd expect."

"Course it is. Any fool could figure that."

Buchanan said, "But it takes a real damn fool to think it out."

"You ain't a real damn fool," said Coco. "You might be a little loco about guns and things, but you're pretty smart sometimes."

"Mind gettin' that map?"

Coco went to Buchanan's saddlebag and brought back the map which he had worn flimsy since Yuma. Breakfast was declared, and they ate thick bacon and stale bread. Charlie had some jerky which he gave them. Buchanan paid him and watched the crestfallen posse depart for home and hearth.

He said, "Farnum keeps going east. And he nudges a bit south until there's danger. Tucson is south and east from Gila Bend. It's got to be in this area." He ran a forefinger round a section of the map.

"There ain't much to pick from, is there?"

"Not much. Tell you what. Let's try and shake Cassidy."

"You mean outguess him or outride him?"

"Both," said Buchanan. "I want a little time. Just enough to be on the ground before Cassidy."

"On account of Mary Jane."

"Right," said Buchanan.

"A lot more hard pushin'."

"Uh-huh."

"And you with that bad shoulder."

"I got you to help."

Coco grinned. "You sure know how to make a man feel good now, don't you, Tom?"

"You may not shoot off guns, old friend, but you're a hell of a man in a fight." Buchanan got up and began to saddle Nightshade. The horse would do, and Buchanan thought the roan that bore Coco was equal to the task. His hunch of the night before was growing in his mind.

He had already picked out the most probable answer, the possible destination.

Cassidy and Snade reined in. The horses, which they had replaced after Farnum had run off the stock of Walton, were not of the top rank. Morgan and Gonzales had fallen behind, not for the first time. Days had passed, and the chase had proven keen.

Snade said, "You sure Buchanan is all that smart?"

"He ain't actin' that way."

"Runnin' around like a chicken with its head cut off. You'd think we were after him to kill him."

"That might happen, damn his soul." They had followed the trail, up hill and down dale, across small streams. Now they were at the edge of shale.

"No use tryin' to follow him across this rocky crap. We ain't got the slightest notion which way he took."

"Them Rangers gone to Tucson."

"There's others scattered all over. Buchanan, he's doublin' and redoublin' like he knows somethin'."

"It don't look to me like he knows what the hell he's up to."

Cassidy said, "He knows, all right. There's been no trace of Farnum whatsoever. Nobody we seen has caught sight of him. And nobody's seen Buchanan or the nigger. How they eatin'? We lose time buyin' or stealin' food. They keep goin'. They got some place in mind, you can bet on it."

"Well, so what's on his mind?"

"I wish to hell I knew."

"Gonzales is out of booze. Morgan's gettin' uneasy-like. You know Morgan."

"He craves somebody to shoot. In the back if possible. Can you handle him?"

"I can keep 'em in line if they see somethin' ahead."

Cassidy debated. "We'll rest awhile. I got to think."

"You're the boss. But you better think quick and good, or it'll be just you and me."

"You're stickin', then?"

Snade said, "I know you a long time, Cassidy. I knew when you was a straight lawman. I was around when you changed your tune and had to get to Walton. I ain't never heard of you crossin' a pardner."

"You never will."

"But you'd cross anybody else. And if you have to kill, you'll kill. Even a gal."

"That's the truth, for fifty thousand."

"So like I said. I may not be the smartest *hombre* in the world, but I ain't dumb. We're in this, and it's a big enough stake to keep goin'."

"That's good enough for me."

"You do your thinkin'. I'll jolly up the boys. Been holdin' out a pint of snakebite medicine. I'll dole some out to Gonzales and tell Morgan all the things he can do with his share of the money."

"You do that, Snade."

He slowly unsaddled his horse. He had never been a man to overreach himself when there was a difficult choice. He thought about the Rangers and their conviction that Farnum would turn up in Tucson. He thought about Buchanan, who surely didn't agree. He thought about the various bounty-hunters, some gathered in

185

small groups, some going it alone. None had arrived at anything, he thought.

And Farnum was the smartest of them all.

Excepting probably Buchanan, he added. Cassidy surmised that Buchanan had deliberately covered his trail; therefore Buchanan had an idea of his own. Cassidy's problem was to work out for himself whatever it was that Buchanan had decided was the right course.

It would take time. He removed his hat and wiped a sweaty brow. Already his head ached.

Farnum sat on a log. It was evening. Conrad was stretched on his blankets, watching the exhausted girl. She was lying on her side, facing them, her eyes closed to slits. Farnum had the notion she was always listening, ever watchful. She had a lot of guts, he thought; she was a great young woman. And Conrad wanted her so bad, it was evident in every move, more and more every day.

It was difficult for Farnum. He had never harmed a woman in his life, and of all people he wished the best for Mary Jane. She had come through the fire. It was the one thing that worried him.

The rest he had all clear. He had planned it from the moment he had known escape was possible. He had honed the plan through the terrible years of his imprisonment. He was on the verge of cashing in.

There had been no sign of pursuit for two days. His route had been roundabout, but he had always made progress toward his destination. He had outfought and outthought the pursuers. Buchanan had not been heard from since the shooting. He wondered if he had killed the great Buchanan. He doubted it. The man had ninety lives, this had been proven. He also did not believe for an instant that Buchanan had given up the chase.

On the other hand, he needed little time once he got his hands on the money. This too he had worked out in his fertile mind. The nearest way station, and they were free. The girl could go back to whatever life held for her.

Excepting that Cole might interfere. He turned over in his mind the possibilities. If Cole made it too hard at the finish—Cole would have to pay the piper. Meantime, Farnum had no alternative but to go on. He could not kill his cousin in cold blood. That would be the easy way, get rid of Cole, take the girl in to the finish and depart with the fifty thousand alone. This was not in his character. Once more he cursed the instinct that had made the cashier draw on him during the robbery.

The men he had killed since rested easy on his conscience. He was no moralist. He had a goal, he had paid a price. Anyone who stood in his way took the consequences.

Conrad broke his train of thought. "We're gettin' near, right, cousin?"

"We're near."

"You been mighty close-mouthed with me about it."

"Didn't want to get your hopes up. That is, not that far up."

"You want to tell me about it now?"

Farnum shook his head. "It'll all be

clear and simple when you see it. Simple as ABC."

Conrad produced his little red juggling balls. He tossed them for a moment or two, absorbed. Then he said, "Fifty thousand. Twenty-five each. That's a fortune. Mary Jane, you know what you can do with that kinda money?"

She closed her eyes tight, pretending to sleep. Both men knew better.

Farnum brooded. In prison he had learned to shut himself off in a world of his own. Now the figure of his cousin intruded, leering at Mary Jane, confusing his thought processes.

There was not much more time. He had worked it out to the finest detail. He had imagined every possible flaw, had eliminated each. He had every belief, every hope that it would go off without a hitch.

There was no Buchanan. And even if there were, Farnum had thought that out, also. Mary Jane was the answer. If Conrad did anything to interfere with that aspect of the plan—could Farnum kill his cousin?

They had been boyhood friends. They were related by blood.

His abnormally sharp ears heard a sound. They had made a cold camp near a copse of piñon trees and he rolled at once toward shelter. Neither Mary Jane nor Conrad moved.

Farnum said, "Stay where you are."

He vanished like a wraith in the night. He poised, rifle in his hands, straining, watching. There was a bit of a moon and a galaxy of stars above the scene.

Conrad whispered loudly, "What's up?"

"Get your gun under the blanket."

Conrad moved with his accustomed celerity. Mary Jane wrapped herself tight in the covering.

Two men rode in. They were heavily armed. One was a halfbreed, the other a big fellow. They dismounted as Conrad greeted them easily, smoothly. "Hi, there."

"Howdy, stranger," said the big man. "You out huntin' Farnum?"

"Everybody's out lookin' for him."

"We lost the trail a ways back. Mind if we squat?"

Conrad said, "We're loners, ourselves. Better you keep goin' along."

The breed got down from his horse. He had a squashed nose and piercing eyes. He walked toward Mary Jane. "Fella no talk, no look," he said. "I look."

He yanked back the blanket. He reached for the bandanna covering Mary Jane's head. He let out a yip when he saw the long hair.

Farnum fired the rifle. The breed fell across Mary Jane. From under cover Conrad fired the revolver. The big man swayed. Farnum's next shot caught him in the side of the head. He dropped from the horse.

Farnum came running. He lifted the corpse from Mary Jane and tossed it aside as if it were a rag doll. He bent close to her. She stared up with wide frightened eyes.

He said softly, "It's all right. Just stay where you are. We'll handle everything."

Conrad was trying to master the two

horses of the dead men. When he had them under control, he took a deep breath.

"You got rabbit's ears, cousin," he said.

"Nice work with the gun," said Farnum.

"It was an easy target."

"Drag 'em into the trees. We'll have to move. There might be some others within hearin'."

"God, I thought at first it was Buchanan," said Conrad.

"He'd never ride in cold like they did," Farnum told him. "Let me look at those horses."

He went over them with care. They were sound, he thought, and they seemed fresh. He began to transfer saddles and gear. Mary Jane sat up, rubbing her eyes, disbelieving. It had been so quiet, so peaceful, and now there were two more dead men. She shook in every limb for a moment or two. It could not be true, but it was true. Dazedly, she went about saddling her own mount, the best of the three they had been riding. Farnum moved with speed and efficiency, cool, always cool. In a short time they were moving on.

Conrad said, riding beside her, "That ain't my game, you know. Never did shoot people. There's other ways most of the time. But when they seen you was a girl it had to be done."

"It had to be done," she said mechanically.

Farnum called back, "Them or us. That's the way of the world. It comes down to them or us."

"They were dumb," said Conrad. "They seen two people and they know there's three of us. Dumb."

"What you see ain't always what you get. Which you have proved plenty times," Farnum agreed. Again he thought of Cole's infatuation with the girl. Again he wondered how it would be at the end, when decisions had to be made on the instant. If Cole made the wrong move they could all be killed, including the girl.

He did not want the girl to die. Not even when they had been successful. He had not lied when he averred that he had never harmed a woman. He had it all figured out that the girl would live, and that he and Cole would escape with the loot.

It had to be his way. It simply could not go any other way. Cole was quick and sly, but there were other things to be considered. He put his mind to work, riding through the night, counting alternatives.

It was morning when Buchanan and Coco came upon the scene at the piñon grove. They had followed trail, by chance it seemed. Or was it, Buchanan wondered, because his hunch was correct? They came in afoot, from opposite sides, and the two abandoned horses grazed on, indifferent, hungry, gaunt.

Buchanan traversed the camp ground and read the story. He pulled the two bodies out into the open. He had no means of digging a hole, but he found blankets to cover them until the next traveler came through. Their saddles gave no clues as to their identity. They were, he supposed, two drifters attracted by the reward money who had blundered upon Farnum.

Reading the tracks, he said, "They rode in, and Farnum bushwhacked them. At least we know which direction he's headed in. Reckon they rode out at night."

"Are we far behind 'em?"

"Far enough."

"We better get 'em soon, or there won't be nobody left in Arizona."

"I'm wondering how far behind Cassidy is right now."

"You figure he's still trailin' us?"

"More or less. Haven't seen hide nor hair of him for a few days. But he's got bulldog in him, seems like."

He picked up a horse dropping. He walked to the eastern edge of the camp.

Coco said, "You know, Tom, they been awful lucky and awful smart. You wouldn't think the good Lord would favor people like him and Conrad now, would you?"

"They get their chances, seems like. They left in the night so they're pushin' hard. Maybe the Lord's givin' 'em enough rope."

"You got it figured, ain't you?"

"Somewhat," said Buchanan. "Farnum's just so damn clever, might be he went a bit too far. What I mean, he's got it down to a nubbin."

"And ain't that good?"

"It is unless somebody gets onto what makes the nubbin." Buchanan's shoulder twinged and he made a face. "He's sure headin' straight for it now. Whatever it is."

"He's outsmarted us some. He hit you in the shoulder. But the gal's still alive. And you got a notion," said Coco.

"He had five and a half years to think it through," said Buchanan. "But actually he thought a heap in the beginning."

"You mean when he stashed the loot?"

"Nobody found it, as we know."

"If you can figure out where it is, then Farnum ain't outsmarted you. Which I was beginnin' to think he had. You, me, Cassidy, all of us."

Buchanan got out the much-thumbed

map. "Here's Picacho Pass, about thirty-eight miles below Picacho Peak. About sixty-eight miles from Tucson. Right near is a new town. Name of Yeager. Somebody diverted some water there and people farmed. Farmers, they ain't like ranchers or sheepmen or any other kinda people."

"I done noticed that," said Coco dryly. "They ain't so much for guns, except for shootin' crows and coyotes and such."

"Farmers fought in the Revolutionary War a heap," said Buchanan. "You mind your history."

"Got no history," said Coco. "I'm a dumb prizefighter."

"That's what some people think, and sometimes you help 'em along. Me, too," Buchanan said.

"This ain't got nothin' to do with Picacho or whatever."

"Yeager," Buchanan said, "Little nothin'-sorta town. Stuck where it is so the farmers can have a general store and such. And a bank."

"A bank? You figure Farnum's goin' all

thisaway to hold up another bank? Tom, you sure you ain't been eatin' loco weed?"

"Yeager," said Buchanan firmly. "There's nothin' near there. Farmers would rather bank handy than tote money to Tucson."

Coco looked at the sky, removed his sombrero, replaced it, spat into the weeds. "If you say so. Any old way there must be some regular feed if there's a general store. Any kind of stuff which is unlike what we been eatin'."

"It's not such a far piece from here," said Buchanan. "Farnum's trail leads in that direction. It's the way I've been thinkin'."

"Smart fellers like you and Farnum, they might be thinkin' alike. Is that it?"

Buchanan said, "It wouldn't be the first time I was wrong. It might be the last."

"Then let's get it over with. Way it is, I'm tired of ridin' and tired of the vittles and tired of Farnum and every other damn thing exceptin' that poor li'l ole gal," Coco said. "If they take her to this here Yeager town, then let's go there."

The trail was plain enough. By the stride of their horses' prints, the fugitives had been in a hurry. Farnum had done his foxy tricks over and over. If he was right, Buchanan thought, the time was for a straight riding with action at the end.

9

MR. and Mrs. Clem Yeager walked down the main street of the town which bore their name. It was nine-forty-five in the morning. The day was sunny. The few people who were in view smiled at the middle-aged couple.

He was fifty years of age. She was forty-five. They had come west from Ohio in the time before there was water, and he had brought water to the arid plain, bringing it down from the high mountains. She had been—and still was—a beauty, once an actress on the stage. For fifteen years she had been part and parcel of her husband and his enterprise.

They had made a good thing of it. They were content and well housed and well fed, and they liked their small town. They dressed well, conservatively, between styles of East and West. They owned the general store, which was managed for them by a man named Zeb Frobish. They had opened a local bank which had proved to be profitable beyond their dreams. They were honest, decent people, respected and liked by all. They had been initially responsible for bringing prosperity to this out-of-the-way place and were justly proud. They had founded a peaceful world of their own and were, in their advancing years, enjoying it to the hilt.

The scattered homes were modest but well built. Local people and itinerant workers lived in them. Miriam and Hiram Agajanian dwelt above the bank in comfortable quarters. The town was an out-of-the-way place with one lawman, free of crime or violence.

They passed the general store, and Zeb came to them with a bill of lading from the company that ran the stage line. There was a small mix-up which Clem straightened out.

Zeb said, "Clem, I couldn't manage without you."

"You could manage. It's just that I'm

convenient." He could tease his friend, he could smile and feel safe. Zeb was another Eastern emigrant, a careful man in all his dealings.

They went on to the bank. The Agajanians had it open. They were a smiling couple of Armenian descent, swarthy and humorous, content with themselves and their son William, a bright boy of ten. He was in the bank, very serious, holding a silver dollar in his hand.

Hiram Agajanian said, "William wants to start an account, Clem. He thinks you should take charge of it. Doesn't trust his parents, I guess."

"Familiarity breeds contempt," said Mrs. Yeager. "William, you should learn to trust your parents."

The boy said, "They taught me not to trust anybody in this world except Mr. Yeager."

"Put not your trust in strangers." Mrs. Yeager smiled sweetly. "And remember, a dollar saved is a dollar earned."

There was no private office in the bank. The two Yeager desks were separated from the Agajanian desks only by a railing. Behind the Yeager desks were a huge iron safe and a smaller chest of steel drawers, secured by padlocks, for the convenience of customers who wished to store valuable items. In the corner near Clem Yeager stood a shotgun. This was the entire furnishing of the private institution.

Clem Yeager sat down behind his desk, Mrs. Yeager went to hers. There was little to do except make out a new account for William. The sun shone through the high rear windows. It was all in all the most pleasant of surroundings on a most pleasant day.

The door opened and a man strode in. Yeager peered at him and said, "Why it's Mr. Jackson."

"How are you?" The man smiled pleasantly.

"Five years ago? My goodness, where have you been?"

"Away," said the man. He was at ease, confident. "You still have my package?"

"The largest in our storage space," said

Yeager. He delved, found a ledger. "I believe you owe us for rent."

"Yeah, I expect so."

"It's quite a large sum. We could compromise. I do not believe in gouging our patrons."

"That's real nice of you." The man produced a revolver. "I don't believe in anything much but my property."

Mrs. Yeager let out a small scream, quickly suppressed. The Agajanians stiffened, frightened. Little William ran cowering to a corner and huddled there.

"You see, I'm short of money," said the man. "Real short. Just hand over the package, please."

He moved so that he was between Yeager and the shotgun leaning against the wall. He reached behind and took hold of the weapon.

Yeager said, "I see we have no choice."

"Just the package."

Yeager arose slowly. He took keys from a hook. He went to the stack of boxes and began comparing numbers. He unlocked one of the largest. He took out a wrapped parcel and put it on his desk.

He said, "There it is, Mr. Jackson. Take it and go."

The man seemed to hesitate. Then he said, "Now the safe. Open it, please."

Both Yeagers stiffened. They looked at each other, at the Agajanians. Then the banker shook his head.

"Mr. Jackson, the people of this town and the farmers in this area came here because of me. If I open that safe they will lose their savings."

Mrs. Yeager said, "And if crops are poor, they would lose everything. Surely, you wouldn't want that to happen, sir."

"I wouldn't." He spoke softly, worriedly. "But I got a partner out there. If we don't take what we can get, there'll be trouble for him and a young lady."

"Are two people more important than a town?"

"Not to you. Only to me. I got a choice here, it seems like. But it only seems like."

Yeager said, "Would you kill me to get the safe open?"

"Maybe."

"I'm the only one who knows the combination," Yeager said. "That is my only precaution. If I die, nobody can open it."

"You mean to say you'd die before you'd open it?"

Yeager drew a deep breath. "I've lived a good life. Some things, sir, are bigger than life."

Mrs. Agajanian cried, "No, Clem, no!"

The boy suddenly ran across the bank. He jumped upon the desk of his mother and clung to her. He did not weep, large eyes stared at the man with the revolver.

The man looked hard at the Yeagers. He saw nothing but calm courage. He looked at the door where an ominous shadow appeared, then vanished.

"Both of you," he said, half to himself. "Man and wife. It would be a bad thing."

Mrs. Yeager said, "Yes, it would be a very bad thing, sir."

The man said slowly, "Would it make a difference if I told you I'm Rube Farnum?"

"I could guess that," Yeager told him. "The Tucson robbery over five years ago. The stories coming in about your escape."

"And you ain't scared?"

"I'm scared."

He looked at the Agajanians. They had now moved together to present a united front. Even the boy stared unwinking at him.

Farnum shook his head. He called out, "Cole! Bring in the dynamite."

Yeager made a small move. Then he stopped. His wife reached out for his hand.

She said, "Better the bank than your life, Clem."

"If I could—" He stopped. His shoulders slumped. "But I cannot. You have the means, Farnum. You have the power. It would be wiser if you took your stolen money and went on."

"Maybe. On t' other hand, every dollar counts where we're goin'." He seemed to be trying to convince himself. They saw his face harden again. "I want to get paid for that five and a half years. Cole wants

207

to have a stake—" He broke off, shaking his head. "I took a lot of lives to get here. It's goin' to take a lot of money to get me clear."

"You're a clever man, Farnum. Depositing the money here." He indicated the package on the desk. "Planning your getaway. Now you're being foolish. There are people out there who will hear an explosion."

"Farmers. That old marshal. We'll handle them. We been handlin' people like them from Yuma to here."

"It's from here on that you have to worry about."

"Let me do the worryin'."

The door opened. Mary Jane came in. Conrad was behind her carrying the box marked XX. The bank people and Mary Jane stared hard at each other with varying emotions. The boy was startled to see a woman.

Mary Jane said faintly, "I'm not with 'em. They took me from Yuma."

"We heard, my dear," said Mrs. Yeager. "We know."

"A hostage," said Yeager. "Again, clever. But not too clever, I fear."

"Who's this jasper with the mouth?" asked Conrad.

"He's the banker," Farnum told him. "Get at that safe if you want the money. See if you can blow it."

"You mean they won't open it?"

"You heard what I said."

"But Rube, we can make 'em open it for us." He put down the box with great care. Smiling, he moved toward the boy and his mother. He produced a folding knife with a long blade.

The boy stepped loose and stood with shoulders hunched, fists doubled. "I ain't scared of you."

Cole Conrad pulled up short, puzzled. Mary Jane let out a little cry and ran between him and the youth.

Farnum said sharply, "That's enough o' that. Get to the safe. Use your brain."

Conrad straightened. His eyes did not leave Mary Jane's. He said, "I was just funnin'. We wouldn't do anything like that."

"Not while I'm alive," she retorted. "If you hurt these people, believe me, I'm goin' down with 'em."

Farnum said, "No need for that."

"We need to rob them," she retorted. "Fifty thousand dollars is yours for the taking. You're bein' pigs."

Conrad interrupted. "We're takin' it, Rube. It's a lead-pipe cinch. The town's asleep out there. They won't know a thing 'til I blow the safe. Then we'll get away fast."

Farnum hesitated. They all hung on his decision. The married couples clung together, hand in hand. The boy moved closer to Mary Jane, still glaring defiance. They were unlike any people Farnum had seen since he'd escaped the jail in Yuma. He surveyed them all, one by one.

Then he sighed and shrugged. "Cole is bein' stubborn. There's things about Cole —okay. Go ahead and do the job."

Conrad bent to the box marked XX. His swift clever fingers moved like spiders, opening, subtracting sticks of dynamite and caps, and stringing a fuse. They watched him, fascinated.

Farnum watched the people. Helpless, they still presented a strangely strong front. Mary Jane was one of them, one of the kind of people he had never known. The effect upon him was strong, but he could not understand it, could not pin it down.

Conrad said, "You mind watchin' the door, Rube? Wouldn't want anybody to come in and start foolishment."

Farnum backed to the door, unslinging his rifle, the revolver steady in his hand. Conrad went to the safe. The local people inside the bank backed away as far as they could from his field of operations. Farnum leaned against the wall and halved his view, his eyes darting from outside to inside, his face hardening again now in the face of action and danger.

Cassidy drew in with Snade beside him. Morgan and Gonzales were rods behind them.

"That damn Buchanan covered his trail

too good. But there's a little town where we can get vittles."

"And booze for Gonzales."

"Wouldn't mind a drink my own self," said Cassidy. "That Buchanan is drivin' me to it."

"What's the name of this burg?"

"Yeager. Just a tiny dot on the map. Farmin' country where there ain't much farmin'. I was through there one time."

Snade asked, "Anything to watch out for?"

"Nothin' but a tired old local lawman, name of Martin. He don't know much. And Yeager, he 'bout owns the town."

"They got a bank?"

"Get that notion outa your head, Snade. Farnum's loot and the rewards if we're smart. It can look clean as a whistle—if we're smart."

"You're smart. I follow you. That's about it."

"Let things run. We'll know how to handle it when the time comes."

They rode a few steps, then Snade asked, "And what if the time don't come?"

"Then we may stop back and see about Yeager's bank. It ain't in my line, but all this time and trouble—somebody's got to pay."

"Just what I was thinkin'."

"Maybe I feel like Farnum," Cassidy said. "He broke outa Yuma, for which I don't blame him none. I broke outa Walton, which was a prison to me."

"I seen enough of it to know what you mean."

"A man goes up and down, and finally he goes around," Cassidy said.

"I been there."

"Them cowtowns I lawed in, they wasn't anything at all. Drunken bums and trail men on the toot. The pay was rotten, and always some son was out to backshoot the man with the star."

"Weren't many Earps, and half of them got it from somebody or other. Masterson, he went to Denver. Saw him in velvet pants workin' a saloon. Luke Short, he made it in Fort Worth. He's about the only one."

"I knew 'em all. Buchanan knew 'em all. You forgot about Buchanan."

"Yeah. How could I forget that bastard?"

"He's somewhere out there. When we leave Yeager, we'll either pick up his trail or run onto Farnum. I ain't give up."

"I know you ain't. That's why I'm stickin' along."

"Let's go, then."

They rode toward Yeager.

Buchanan reined in, and, wincing at the pain in his shoulder, leaned down. Coco rode beside him.

Buchanan said, "I be damn. Track's plain as the nose on your face."

Coco rubbed his slightly flattened nose. "That ain't so plain."

"It is to me. They rode into that little old town. I had a notion about that town."

"How long ago did they get here?"

"Not too long. Tracks' fresh."

Coco said, "What we waitin' for?"

"For takin' care. We go to the edge of

214

the burg. Then we tie up the horses. Then we sneak in."

"Like they may be layin' in wait for us?"

"They didn't bother to cover back-trail."

"Maybe they was in a hurry."

"I do believe that. Uh-huh, it's part of my thinkin'."

"How come?"

"They're gettin' near the cache for the loot. When Farnum gets in a hurry, means he's comin' close."

"That's what you been thinkin' on?"

"This here town. Almost didn't find it on the map. Figure the time he was loose after robbin' the Tucson bank."

"You sure he come this way with the loot?"

"I ain't been sure of anything since we started on this chase," said Buchanan. "Otherwise I wouldn't have taken a bullet in my carcass. But I got a hunch."

They rode to the town of Yeager. On the outskirts, they found an abandoned shack big enough to tie up the horses in such fashion that they would not be seen from the road. Buchanan affixed his revolver belt and slung his rifle. Coco spat on his hands, and they began the walk down the main street.

At the edge of town, as though hidden and unwanted, was a building, upon which a sign read, "Marshal Martin. Jailhouse." A man slept in a tilted chair. Buchanan went to him, touched his shoulder. Bleary eyes opened, stared, were knuckled.

"Tom Buchanan!"

"Howdy, Milt."

"Where in tarnation you come from?"

"Up north a ways," said Buchanan. "You been out here nappin' very long?"

"It's about all I do, except nip a little and sleep a lot. Nothin' ever happens here."

Coco said sharply, "Looky yonder, Tom."

Buchanan looked. He saw the horses tied up at the building halfway down the street. He asked, "Did you see those people come into town? Two men and a gal?"

Martin said, "Nope."

Coco said, "It's them, all right."

"And they're inside. What's in that place, Martin?"

"That's the bank. Yeager's bank. He's boss around here, sorta, 'ceptin' he's a right nice kinda boss to have."

"A bank, eh? And those three people are inside."

"Lots of people come to do business with Clem Yeager. He's a good man."

Buchanan said, "These people didn't come to do any kind of business good for him, nor the town neither."

The marshal arose. He was bent, with the hump of the aged on his back. His eyes had become bright, however. He touched the big gun he was wearing, touched his star of office. "Bank robbers?"

"Worse," Buchanan told him. "Farnum and Conrad and the gal they kidnapped in Yuma."

"I heard about that. On the telegraph. I swan. We better git down there."

"How many people would be in the bank?" asked Buchanan.

"Well, there's Mr. and Mrs. Yeager. And the Agajanians, they work there. Them, at least."

"We don't go down there," said Buchanan. "Farnum and Conrad have already got one hostage. We'll let 'em do whatever, and then we'll nail 'em comin' out. That way we can worry only about the gal."

Martin considered. "Well, we might get acrost the street and hide out. The smithy, he's almost directly opposite from the bank."

"Lead the way," said Buchanan. "Around the back so that nobody sees us. Can you keep the street clear?"

"I'll talk to a couple people. Ain't many lives here, y'know. Mainly they come in from the farms and all. Sat'day nights the place almost comes alive."

"If somethin' goes wrong right now, it'll come alive. And next thing people will be dead," said Buchanan grimly.

"Farnum, he's a bad one," agreed Martin. "Killed some on the way. I wonder why he come off the trail to here. It don't seem reasonable."

"Uh-huh. Farnum ain't reasonable. Neither is his cousin, Conrad. Let's get started around the back ways."

The old man moved with a lurching but strong stride. Hitching up his Levis, he led them through backyards and quickly across empty spaces between the houses. The blacksmith shop was open on both ends. They slid inside.

The smithy was a short, wide man named Bud Meany. He was startled at their entrance, pausing with hammer in hand, a hot horseshoe on the anvil. A farm animal was docile, waiting patiently to be shod.

Martin said, "Jest holt steady, Bud. These are friends o' mine. You seen anything peculiar acrost at the bank?"

"I ain't seen anything but this horse's rear end and the fire and the bellows," said the blacksmith. "Got to get 'er done for Brown. You know how feisty he is. Only mean man in this here valley when it comes to his hosses."

Buchanan said, "Damn the curtains on those windows." He was staring at Yeager's bank. "Can't see inside."

"Miz Yeager sets great store by them curtains," said Martin. "Got two sets. Keeps 'em neat and clean all the time."

"Keep out of sight as much as you can," said Buchanan. "When they come out just leave it to me."

"I could deputize you," said Martin. "Make it all legal-like."

"I don't need deputizin'," said Buchanan. "Main thing is that the gal don't get hurt. Nor anyone else if we can help it. But Farnum's quick with his rifle. If he makes the wrong move take your shot."

"I ain't shot at nobody for ten years," said Martin.

"Is there a back way out of the bank?" asked Buchanan.

"That's the way to the outhouse," said Martin.

"Uh-huh. Supposin' you and the smithy here and whoever else you can get take a position back of the outhouse. Farnum is a medium-sized strong fella, Conrad is thin and—well, ordinary. But if they try to take out the girl, hold your fire. Understood?"

"We let 'em go with the gal? Loot and all?"

"Whatever," said Buchanan. "Just shoot off your rifle three times quick. That'll be our signal."

Coco said, "We been chasin' 'em for too long. But we'll chase 'em forever rather than hurt the gal."

"Sure, I agree," said the marshal. "Money ain't nothin' compared to lives. But they got good people in there. What about them?"

"Somethin' we got to fret about," Buchanan told him. "This ain't goin' to be no easy thing."

"How about their horses?"

"What good are they with us standin' watch? Wish they would take to the horses. We could pick 'em off without hittin' Mary Jane."

Buchanan looked around the shop. The double door was wide open to the street.

He would have given a lot to be able to see behind the curtains of the bank directly opposite.

He said, "That anvil. Can it be moved?"

"If you got the muscle," said the smithy.

"Coco?"

"Sure enough."

Buchanan and Coco approached the anvil. At the last moment, just as they were lifting it, the smithy came to lend a hand. They placed it strategically in the middle of the opening.

"Those bags of coal and sand," Buchanan suggested. "If we heap 'em alongside the anvil, it'll give us a nice spot."

It was done. They moved with great haste and great care. Buchanan was satisfied. He waved the marshal and the smithy to their appointed places.

He said to Coco, "Give 'em plenty of time. Old Martin don't move very fast, and he's got to arm the smithy. And maybe pick up some help."

"Farnum wouldn't go out the back way and leave his horses."

"Farnum ain't going to have much choice."

"Unless he gits us. You know what a helluva shot he is."

"He is, at that. But if he shows his head at this range he'll be good and dead. Just so we don't harm Mary Jane."

They waited, crouching, watching the bank. Buchanan wondered how long they had been there. Something must have gone wrong or they would have appeared by now, he decided. He thought of walking across the street and into the building. Were it not for Mary Jane he probably would have done so. His shoulder still ached, but his right arm was unharmed. He could handle the revolver at close quarters—his mind ran on, but he knew there was only one thing to do. They had to wait and take their chances when Farnum and Conrad came from the bank.

Coco said, "It's takin' 'em a real long time to get it done."

"Just what I was thinking," said

Buchanan. "Martin and the others are at the back door by now. If they spot him it'll be all hell to pay."

"Reckon Martin and them'll keep their heads down. Reckon they ain't got too much stomach for this."

"Let's hope so." Waiting, as always, was the hardest part.

Cassidy was unhappy. "This damn wagon road don't show track I can read. Gonzales!"

The Mexican got down from his horse. He was not quite steady. He had been drinking until the bottle was empty, bored with the entire proceeding. He knelt and nosed around, shook his head, clambered back on his horse.

Morgan said, "The hell with it. We gotta eat."

Snade said, "Yeah, Yeager's right ahead. Let's go in quiet and get some food."

"What if Buchanan is waitin' for us?"

"I'll shoot off his goddam head," said Morgan.

"That's been tried before. Lotsa times," said Cassidy. "Don't start nothin' with Buchanan. Palaver will do better."

"You scared of him?" Morgan's thin lips curled, twisting his slight chin. "Seems to me you're godawful careful of him."

"Scared?" Cassidy looked at the slim youth. He suddenly reached out, swung a long arm. Morgan flew from the saddle and hit the ground, one side of his face scarlet. "Now you claim to be the fastest gun alive. Am I scared of you?"

Morgan rolled over, dusted himself off. His eyes were like hot irons. He got back in the saddle. He shut his mouth tight and stared into the distance.

Snade said, "You better watch it, Morgan. Me and Cassidy, we got our eye on you. Forget the fast draw, son. It got better men than you into Boot Hill."

Gonzales announced, "Want tequila."

"We'll ride into town and ask around," said Cassidy. "I don't like it we ain't found trail on either Farnum nor Buchanan. I don't like it a damn bit."

"It's a big country," Snade said. "Too damn big. But they got to be somewhere between here and Tucson."

"Talk about a needle in a damn haystack," muttered Cassidy. "Only thing to do is keep on into town. They got a telegraph office. Leastways we can get the latest from the Rangers and all."

"Ain't seen a Ranger. Reckon they went to Tucson and started fannin' out. Back-trackin', maybe, the way Farnum might have went."

"They got enough men. All we can do is mosey along." It was very unsatisfactory but he knew no alternative. They resumed their course.

There was motion across the street, and Farnum could see part of it. When the anvil and the bags were put in place, he said nothing. He recognized Buchanan and Coco; the other man was obviously the blacksmith. Still, he debated. There was no use alarming Cole, who was jittery enough, handling the dynamite, placing it where it would spring the hinges of the iron safe. There was no use raising the hopes of the hostages and Mary Jane. It was coming down to a point when it would depend upon him, upon his reasoning, his actions.

They could not now go out the door and ride away, that was certain. He turned away and looked at the others, keeping his face expressionless. It made no difference now whether they got the money from the safe.

He said quietly, "Cole, can you come here a minute?"

The Yeagers and Agajanians and the boy were crowded against the wall farthest from the safe. Mary Jane was with them. He had meant to make them all crawl under the desk when the charge was set off. He had not meant to harm them. Now he was in a different position. Now he would have to make up his mind who was to be sacrificed.

He nodded to the curtains and said, "Be careful. Don't let them see you."

"Let them see me? Let who see me?"

"Across the street. Buchanan and the black man."

Cole peeked past an edge of a curtain without disturbing it. He stepped back. "You saw them?"

"Just a couple moments ago."

"Jeez."

"The back way will be covered, never fear. Our horses are covered."

"We can still blow the safe and make 'em let us get away. We got more'n the girl now. We got plenty people they won't want to hurt. We'll take Mary Jane and go."

"You blow the safe and Buchanan'll be in here. Then one of us or both of us will get it."

"But we'll get him."

"Maybe."

"No maybe about it."

"When the safe blows, there'll be stuff fallin' down on us. Ceiling, walls maybe. You don't know about dynamite in indoors. It ain't a sure thing. You don't know that much about it."

"I still say—"

"And dynamite's a weapon if used right. I learned that in Yuma, cousin. No, you don't blow the safe. Lucky you didn't already do it. Now get the sticks and put caps on them."

Conrad said, "There's only one way outa here. Put the people in front, get to the horses with Mary Jane and ride."

"That may be."

"What else?"

"A lot is up to Buchanan."

"He ain't that tough nor smart. There's got to be a way out of here. We came this far, we can go the rest of the way."

"With Mary Jane?"

"We couldn't do it without her. Buchanan would never let her be hurt."

"And if she goes with us she won't be harmed in any way. Is that it, Cole?"

There was just a speck of hesitation. Then he said, "Of course not. Sooner or later we turn her loose."

Farnum did not respond. The girl stood with the local prisoners, straining to hear. She was a brave one, he thought, and smart, too. There would be a risk no matter which way it went. If she had the slightest chance she would make a break for it. And she had come to fear Cole more than she did himself.

Cole said, "I tell you, it can be done. We talk to Buchanan. He's waitin' for us to talk to him. He's got to know we're in here account of the horses. He's got to have it figured out, hasn't he?"

"Oh, yes," said Farnum. "Buchanan knows it all by now. He would not have come here if he hadn't figured it somehow or other. That's the trouble. Buchanan is the only man who ever thought along with me."

Conrad raised his voice, "Mary Jane will talk to him. Won't you, Mary Jane?"

She stood tall among the people surrounding her. She said, "No. You're not going to use me like that."

Yeager said calmly, "I'll talk to whoever you want. I don't know what's going on, but I'll be the go-between."

Farnum said, "We haven't heard from him yet."

"We will," said Conrad. "It's best to

deal with him before somebody else gets into town."

"That's true," Farnum agreed.

Mary Jane said with scorn, "Why don't you talk to him yourselves, you brave men?"

"And get our heads shot off?" demanded Conrad.

She turned to the other hostages. "They don't mean to let me go. You can see that. They're going to take me along to keep them safe."

Yeager stroked his chin. Agajanian scowled. The boy stared with hatred at the captors. The women huddled together in the corner. There was a silence in the little bank. It was broken by the sound of hooves and harness from the street outside.

A voice yelled, "That's them! That's their hosses. They're in the damn bank!"

Farnum peered from behind the curtain. He said, "Four hard cases. It's that bunch from Walton."

"Where we ran off their stock?"

"The same," said Farnum. "Listen!"

Now the stentorian voice of Buchanan roared, "Right there, Cassidy. Don't make any moves."

"Stalemate," murmured Farnum. "It's dog-eat-dog from here on out. Keep your heads down, everybody. These jaspers don't respect man, woman nor child."

They all made themselves as small as possible. Farnum continued to peek out the window. Again the silence fell. Farnum held his rifle and kept the watch.

Buchanan stood behind the anvil in the doorway in the blacksmith shop. The four horsemen were lined up in the street. Coco was out of sight at the moment.

Cassidy yelled, "The hell with you, Buchanan. We got 'em."

Morgan reined his horse around. Without words he reached for his revolver. Buchanan's right hand did not seem to move. His six-gun belched.

Morgan reeled. His drawn Colt dropped from his hand. He fell from the saddle. His spur caught in the stirrup. The horse bolted, dragging the chinless young man out of town.

The sound of the shots sent the mounts of Cassidy, Snade and Gonzales bolting. Buchanan spun around, then held his fire. Grimacing, he shook his head.

"I never could get to shootin' people in the back," he said. "Now the fat is in the sizzlin' damn fire."

There was a tinkle of glass. A window of the bank broke outwards. The barrel of a rifle appeared.

Buchanan shouted, "Farnum, don't be a damn fool. We got to talk."

Farnum's voice came clear and calm. "That's right, Buchanan. But them fellas, they don't want to talk."

"All the more reason," Buchanan called. "You give us the girl and the other people, we give you a head start."

"On your word?"

"My word."

"Gladly taken. But what about the other people?" asked Farnum. "How you goin' to get them to agree?"

"That's somethin' I haven't figured out. Just want to get it straight between you and us, Coco and me."

"I'll take that for granted," Farnum said. "Now you got to figure out the rest of it. And if Cassidy wants to try and take us, let him."

"Can't do that while you got Mary Jane."

"That's what I reckoned," said Farnum. He spoke as if they were in a friendly saloon, discussing a deal for cattle or pigs or sheep. "It's your wagon, Buchanan."

"Thanks a whole lot," he replied. He watched as the rifle barrel was withdrawn. He stepped forward and craned to peer in the direction taken by Cassidy and his remaining two cohorts. A bullet was his answer, not too close, a warning shot.

He said, "Cassidy's holed up. The houses are so far apart in this town, he's probably in an alley. Out of range of Farnum, of course. Keep an eye on the back door, Coco."

"I'll be watchin' for him. Reckon he won't be comin', though. Not when he seen what you did to that skinny fella."

"Guns," said Buchanan. "You don't like guns."

"I don't like *him* having one, neither."
Coco debated for a moment. "Course if
there *is* guns, just as well you be the
quicker."

Farnum called out through the broken
window. "You see what I mean,
Buchanan? They'd gun you down quick
as they would me. Now what's on your
mind?"

"There's people behind the bank. You
know that. You think they'll stay there?"

"Ain't one of 'em in sight. They'll stay."

Cassidy's voice cut in, uncomfortably
close. "You two ain't got all the say. I'm
the law. I call on you to surrender,
Farnum, you and Conrad. Come out with
your hands up."

"Now that's funny," said Farnum
conversationally, addressing Buchanan.
"We got a passel of people in here. We
got Mary Jane. And he wants us to give
up."

"You got no food and water," Cassidy
yelled. "We can starve you out, man."

"You'll have to do better'n that,"
Farnum said. "We ain't waiting to starve."

Buchanan took his turn. "If you try to charge in there, Cassidy, you're a dead man. You already lost one careless *hombre*. You want to try for three more?"

"That's throwin' in with Farnum," howled Cassidy. "You're goin' agin the law, Buchanan."

"If you're the law, so be it," Buchanan told him.

There was no one in view. The citizens of Yeager had taken to positions of safety, apart from the three-cornered battle. Buchanan maintained his stand. Coco squatted down, watching the rear. Someone would have to make the first move. Someone would die, Buchanan knew. Farnum would not allow a long siege, because he could not afford it. Any moment another force of manhunters might arrive, either by accident or design.

Coco said, "I don't see how you're gonna figure this one, Tom, I truly don't. That Cassidy's got three guns. Farnum's got two. How we gonna get out of this here rangdoodle?"

"Patience is a virtue, my daddy used to

say. Although I never knew it to get to a point. If it wasn't for Cassidy I could deal. This way, we got to figure how to make some kind of break."

"You better think about it. I already got a headache," said Coco.

"I'm thinkin'," Buchanan told him. "Not gettin' anywhere, but still, I'm thinkin'."

He settled down for a brief wait. If Cassidy made the break it would be all over. Farnum would take care of at least two of them, and Buchanan could handle the third. Cassidy, he thought, was smart enough not to put his neck in that noose. How smart was he? That was the question.

Inside the bank, Mary Jane was also thinking hard. Three women and a boy, two men who were not fighters, no water, no food—and two desperate, trapped criminals—oddly, her mind sharpened under this pressure. She watched the boy and saw that like all kids he had also recovered from his first alarm. He sidled near her and clutched her hand, silent but sharp-eyed.

Farnum was saying, "Cassidy could try ricochet shots. If you'll all move over to this side, closer to the front of the building, it'll be better for you."

They moved, like cattle she had seen choused by a cowboy. The boy clung to her, still wide-eyed and alert. The others seemed stunned by the shots outside in the street.

Farnum told them, "One of the new bunch under Cassidy tried to draw on Buchanan. He's dead."

Conrad muttered, "I'm fast, but I never saw such hands."

"Every man to his trade." Farnum appeared calm, but Mary Jane knew he was seething beneath the surface. "We could have dealt with Buchanan. Now this Cassidy, he wants us dead or alive."

"We could break out the back way. People won't kill their own friends," said Conrad.

"Those people ain't experienced with

238

guns," said Farnum. "They're liable to kill anybody they see."

"Damn it, we could hide behind these people we got here."

"And Mary Jane?"

Once more the cunning eyes came her way. She felt the impact, and when he was silent she knew Conrad had not given up his design upon her. She shivered. She racked her brain for some kind of escape plan, something she could start herself.

Conrad had been fiddling with the dynamite. He had attached caps and fuses to several sticks. He now bound them together with wire.

"We could chuck this out back. Then make a run for it."

Farnum shook his head. "No sure way to reach 'em before someone shot us."

"We got to take some kind of chance."

"The horses are out front," Farnum said. "On foot they'd have us in a jiffy."

"If we could reach Cassidy and them with a bomb—"

"Buchanan's got us covered."

"He won't shoot whilst we got Mary Jane and these folks."

"Don't bet on it," said Farnum. "Never bet on what he'll do."

Conrad fell silent, but Mary Jane could almost see the wheels going around in his head. He was more schemer than fighter, she thought, and therefore twice as dangerous.

Farnum said, "The dynamite. It's the only thing'll get us out of here. Got to figure how."

"The roof?" suggested Conrad. He looked upward. There was a safety hatch. The ladder leaned in a corner. He brought it over and set it under the trap door.

"Show your head, and it'll be blown away," Farnum said.

"I was thinkin' of sendin' one of these people up there. Maybe the kid, here."

The Agajanian boy faced him. "I won't go."

"Oh, you'd go if I said I'd shoot your ma," Conrad said carelessly. He had, Mary Jane thought, come close to the edge. People changed under stress, she realized. What she had thought about Farnum and Conrad no longer held the full truth. She felt the boy tremble even as he defied them.

She said, "If anyone shows any part of themselves, Cassidy will shoot. You saw what happened, Farnum. You saw his man killed by Buchanan."

Farnum said, "She's right. This is like a fort surrounded by Injuns. We got to figure that's it, that's the way it is and it ain't goin' to change."

"Then we got to go out blazin'," said Conrad. "With dynamite sticks. It's our only chance. We can't hole up here, it ain't healthy."

Farnum nodded. "It a possibility. Cole, I ain't sayin' there's another way."

There was a crackle of glass. The first bullets from Cassidy, Snade and Gonzales came in on an angle, splattering into the wall. The unarmed citizens ducked beneath the desks. Only Mary Jane and the boy stood firm against the wall, watching Farnum and Conrad. Neither returned the fire, knowing the uselessness because of the position of Cassidy and his men.

Were there worse things than death? Mary Jane wondered. What would it be like to go into the blackness? She had no firm religion. She did not know what she believed. She only knew she did not want to die.

Cassidy was reloading his rifle. Snade and Gonzales did the same. Then they heard Buchanan's voice.

"Cassidy?"

"The hell with you."

"There's women and a boy in there."

"Who gives a damn? You ain't runnin' this, Buchanan."

"You're askin' for a heap of trouble. If you harm any of those folks you got the town on your back."

"You lemme worry about that, Buchanan. This town don't mean a damn to me now."

"And you're the lawman? You're a thief and a fool, Cassidy."

"And you're Buchanan. Let's see you get out of this one, Buchanan."

Nevertheless he nursed his rifle, scowling. Snade came and sat beside him. They were in an alley, as Buchanan had predicted, between two houses from which the residents had promptly and wisely fled. Gonzales sat on his heels and said nothing.

Snade peered out, then ducked back. "Looks like we got us a three-cornered zinger here."

"There's fifty thousand dollars in that bank, you can bet. Farnum wouldn't be tryin' to rob it, not this time. And whatever is in the safe. That's a heap of cash, Snade."

"You think I ain't got my mind on it? I also seen Morgan try to outdraw Buchanan."

"If we could get Buchanan from the back, we could take the bank."

"I ain't about to try that. He's got that big nigger in there with him. Buchanan won't leave his back open."

"I believe you." Cassidy debated. The thought of the immense amount of cash

243

was overwhelming. He could taste it, and it tasted better than any flavor he had ever imagined. "There's got to be a way. Farnum's hedged in. Damn! If we could make a deal with Buchanan, it might work. Let the gal go, all that."

"If Morgan hadn't drawed on him—and you hadn't told him off—now I don't know," said Snade. "Man like Buchanan, he thinks different."

"Morgan or no Morgan, he wouldn't let us take the bank like we should," said Cassidy. "Seems like we got to get Buchanan before he makes his move."

"What move? There's three of us and two of them. He can't make no move."

"Two of 'em. Sure. Buchanan and that nigger prizefight champion. You let the black one near you and guns won't help. I know about them two."

"Then what?" demanded Snade.

Gonzales snored. Cassidy shook his head. He lapsed into silence, leaning on his rifle.

The sun was westering. An uncanny

silence had fallen on the town of Yeager. Buchanan moved uneasily, scowling, his freckles hard against his florid flesh.

"Coco, we can't wait 'til dark. This has to be done right and done quick."

"Cassidy could sneak up in the dark," agreed Coco.

"I can't leave here for fear he'd make some damfool move."

"No use, I can't handle no gun."

"I wouldn't ask you. What we've got to do is talk to Farnum where Cassidy can't hear."

"You mean I got to do it?"

"You can do it. I'll cover you as you go out the back door."

"What I goin' to say?"

"Tell Farnum our offer still stands."

"You mean let the people and Mary Jane go, and we'll give him a start?"

"You reckon he'll believe us?"

"It's a chance."

"Then what we do about Cassidy and them?"

"Talk to the people out back of the

245

bank. Get them to agree in order to save their townfolk."

"And let 'em out the back of the bank?"

"It's all I can think of right now."

Coco thought it over. He said, "I don't know if they'll listen to a black man. You know how they are."

"This ain't a hard-boiled town. This is a country town. You make 'em listen. You're the champ."

Coco said, "I dunno. Right now I don't feel like champeen of nothin'."

"But you'll do it."

"Oh, sure. I'll do it. I know you're right, we got to make the move." He opened and closed his big, scarred hands. "Talkin' to white folks ain't my way. But I'll try."

"Just talk straight. Some people can tell honesty when it walks up and bites 'em. Explain about Cassidy. Then tell Farnum and Conrad to git."

"But without Mary Jane."

"Without anybody but them two and their loot."

"Their horses is out front."

"Ask the marshal to get them horses."

"Tom, that's a helluva big order."

"I know it."

"It'll take time."

"That's what I need. Time to make Cassidy nervous, get him off-balance."

"Three of them. One of you. And Farnum layin' over there, him and Conrad both ready to shoot."

"That's my problem," said Buchanan. "You want to try it?"

"Nope," said Coco. "But I'm a-goin' to."

Buchanan went to the rear of the shop. "When I step out you run. Get to the last house, then duck across the street. That's when there may be danger. Just keep runnin' low."

"I'm moanin' low," said Coco. He crouched like a sprinter on the mark.

Buchanan stepped out into the open, rifle cocked. Coco ducked and ran. He was as fast afoot as any man in the country, and now caution led wings to his heels. No one showed himself and Buchanan stepped back into the smithy, drawing a long breath. He had to take a mid-position, now, so that he could keep watch on both front and back.

He knew Coco, knew his courage and his integrity. He also was well aware of the charm the black champion possessed. The charm came from his complete, innate honesty. If any plea could have its effect he was sure that Coco could bring it off. The fear was that Cassidy would make a break to get into the bank and get himself killed along with innocent people. It was a situation over which he, for once, felt no control. Everything depended upon the action of others. Somehow, he knew, he would have to get atop the proceedings. Nothing in his experience proffered help. He settled down to that which he most hated—more waiting.

Inside the bank building, Conrad, peering past the curtains at the rear window, exclaimed, "Coco just ran to join them local people."

Farnum came to look. "Buchanan's making a move."

"What kinda move? He's alone over yonder now. He can be backshot."

"Didn't you tell me Coco wouldn't have any part of guns?"

"That's right. He purely hates 'em."

"Then it's a peaceful errand, ain't it?"

"Who the hell knows?" Once more Conrad's nerves were scraping the surface of his skin. "Who knows anything? Maybe we ought to jump out and take our chances."

"What chances? Our horses are covered. Wonder they haven't shot them down by now."

Conrad indicated the dynamite. "Let me throw a couple of these. If we're lucky, we can get away when they go off."

"Luck! If we depended on luck, we'd still be in Yuma. You on the outside, me on the inside. Oh, no. Never push your luck. I want to see what Coco's up to."

Mary Jane sighed. Conrad would have ended it all. He would have died in a blast of loud noise and foolish risk. Farnum was too clever for it, by far. He held onto the boy and stayed against the wall. The

Yeagers and the Agajanians had recovered from the initial shock and were standing up to it like brave people. If one little thing went wrong, they would all die, Mary Jane knew.

They heard the voice of Coco. They looked out and saw him, waving a more or less white rag. He came within fifty yards and waited. He stood foursquare, patently unarmed, steady and calm and unafraid.

Farnum poked his rifle barrel through the window. "What you want, Coco?"

"Give you a way out. These people agree." He kept his voice low but they could hear him.

"Just you and your money," Coco said. "No Mary Jane. No nobody. Tom Buchanan, he couldn't allow that. Two horses and a head start."

"Who's gonna keep Cassidy from gunnin' us down as we go?"

Coco waved a hand. "These good folks —and Buchanan."

"There's three of them left over yonder. They're killers. They won't give us a start."

"You got to leave that to Buchanan and me," Coco said earnestly. "You got to trust somebody, don't you? Can't stay in there forever. We can eat and drink. You got nothin'. Tom's concern is not to get no good people killed. You ought to know that your own selves."

"Cassidy won't stop."

"You got to believe we can stop him, somehow or t'other."

Conrad whispered, "I don't like it. We take Mary Jane. Otherwise Buchanan'll run us down like he done before."

Farnum did not answer him. He said to Coco, "It's an offer. We got to think on it."

"Would expect you to," said Coco. "Ain't got the hosses for you yet. But don't take too much time. Come night, anything can happen. You know that."

"I know it. Okay, Coco. Thanks for the try."

"That mean you ain't gonna do it?"

"Like I said, it means I'll think on it."

"Think fast, Mr. Farnum," said Coco

quietly and seriously. "You ain't got that much time."

He turned and walked back to where the local posse was hidden. His step was firm, his head high.

Conrad said, "You should see that son fight. He's a champ, all right."

"Horses. The money," said Farnum. He looked at Mary Jane, then at Conrad. "You satisfied?"

"No. But I don't see no other way with Buchanan and Cassidy out front."

"You keep the dynamite handy in case."

"You know it, cousin."

"It's our only chance."

"Buchanan's notion. No doubt about that."

"Course it's Buchanan's notion. That's why I feel like it might work."

Mary Jane breathed naturally for the first time in weeks. Conrad was staring, but she could endure the gaze now that the decision was made. She could feel the relaxation of the others in the bank. It was now impossible for Conrad to blow the safe. The local savings were not threatened. If the pair got away from Yeager, there would still be Buchanan to trail them. But not Cassidy, she thought. Buchanan and Cassidy could not travel the same trail on the same mission for much longer. She felt it in her bones.

Conrad was making a pair of tight packages of the money, using stiff paper he'd found. He fashioned a heavy paper sack, and in it he placed with great care the sticks of capped dynamite. He produced a long, thin cigarillo, and with his usual dexterity placed matches in a row alongside it—and close to the dynamite.

"Ready any time," he told Farnum.

He had the rifle which Farnum had for one moment relinquished while talking with Coco. He was smiling thinly. His eyes were glazed.

Farnum said, "Now you wait, Cole."

He shook his head. "You run things good when we're movin' outdoors. You been runnin' me all my life. You forget you'd still be in jail if it wasn't for me."

"I forget nothin'," said Farnum. Even now he showed no excitement, no fear.

"We've got one chance and that's to go out back, get away and carry out my plan."

"Without Mary Jane. Without the money in the safe."

"With fifty thousand dollars. Which I stole. Half is yours. You never had twenty-five thousand in your life, Cole. You don't know what it means."

"I say we do it my way. We blow the safe. We grab the money. We go out front and take Mary Jane."

"You want to fight Buchanan and Cassidy?"

"Cassidy is a fool. Buchanan will cut him down pronto. We'll get the other two easy. I saw that gunslinger draw and I saw Buchanan draw. I'm quicker, cousin, never forget it." He held out his hand. "We do this my way."

Farnum said, "You'll get one of us or all of us killed."

"They'll charge when they hear the safe explode," Cole said. "I know Buchanan. I know his ways. He'll come a-runnin', and I'll blast him. The rest is easy."

Mary Jane spoke suddenly, "You're

crazy. I won't go with you. Not to save my life."

"You'll go. Or you will die. I don't aim to live without you, Mary Jane." He drew himself up to his inconsiderable height. "All this time we been together. Can't you see? Us, we're smart. You the best gal I ever did know. You and me, we can be rich, we can go anyplace, do what we want to do."

"What you want to do don't interest me," she said.

"You'll learn, gal. Now I'm goin' to give Rube just a minute to go along. Then I'm goin' to blow this safe and do what I got to do."

"You were always a fool," Farnum said sadly. "Quick with the hands, slow with the mind."

"I'll show you who's a fool!"

He reached with the glowing end of the cheroot, his eyes mad. He touched the fuse leading to the safe.

Farnum said, "They'll shoot our horses, you fool."

The people in the bank crowded

beneath the desks. The boy now ran to his mother and curled there on the floor. Only Mary Jane stood erect, against the wall, defiant. The fuse sizzled, the flame marching toward the big safe.

"You think I'm dumb?" demanded Conrad. He picked up two sticks of dynamite he had wired together. He went to the window which was broken open. He again lit a fuse with the tip of his cigarillo. He tossed the explosive over the horses, at the blacksmith shop. It landed in the wide open front of the shop.

"Now see what happens," he shouted. "Now see if I'm the dumb one!"

Cassidy was watching. He saw the dynamite arch on its course. He shouted, "They're blowin' up Buchanan! Now we git 'em."

He led Snade and Gonzales from the alley. He ran directly across the street, keeping as clear as possible of the explosion to come. He waited one second for the blast.

Coco came running into the smithy,

saying, "They agreed to it, Tom. It's—"
He stopped short digging in his heels.

Buchanan was holding a dynamite bomb
in his hands. The fuse, rather long, was
sputtering. He had experienced much with
dynamite in his time. He looked across the
street and said, "Cassidy's makin' his play.
Better keep your head down."

"You playin' Fourth of July with that
there thing?"

"Just timin' it for what it's goin' to do,"
said Buchanan.

He turned and drew back his arm and
threw it across the street. He picked up
his rifle and watched, kneeling behind the
anvil.

The dynamite never came within reach
of Cassidy or his friends. It went off in
midair. Snade and Gonzales screamed.
There was a cloud of smoke and dust.
They went down.

Miraculously, Cassidy, forewarned,
leaped clear. He staggered, running for the
bank. At that moment the charge in the
safe of the bank went off. Flying glass

greeted Cassidy as he arrived at the door. He staggered back.

Buchanan said, "Somethin' loco's going on."

He began running across the street. At any moment he thought Farnum would shoot him once more, this time fatally. He zigged and zagged. Through the billowing smoke he saw Cassidy aiming at him. He threw a quick shot.

Cassidy rolled over, flung out his arms. He landed on his hands, sank slowly, lay prone upon the walk.

Another huge leap and Buchanan was inside the bank. It was afire, the flames licking the wall behind the safe, the door of which lay open. Two men were struggling. Mary Jane was on the floor, moving in a daze.

Coco ran past Buchanan and picked up the girl as if she were a bag of feathers. He ran back into the street.

Buchanan went forward. Now he could dimly distinguish Farnum and Conrad fighting over a rifle.

He said, "Okay, it's all over, boys."

"Damned if it is!" cried Conrad.

His finger found the trigger and pulled it. Farnum fell back. Conrad spun around. The rifle was pointed at Buchanan.

"I'll show 'em who's dumb!" he yelled.

Buchanan shot him in the leg. He fell back. The rifle described a parabola. Buchanan caught it in midair.

The smoke eddied. People moaned. The charge had been too great. Pieces of iron and furniture had splattered around the small room. Buchanan went to Conrad and put his foot upon a hand still reaching for a weapon.

Conrad said, "I thought I was quicker than you."

"Whoever called you dumb had his head on straight," said Buchanan. He dragged the man into the street. Now the local people were straggling out. Marshal Martin came puffing around the corner of the bank building.

Buchanan said, "Take care of this one. Watch him close."

Martin held his old-fashioned long-barreled Colt .45 in his hand. "He makes a move, he'll be gone. What happened in there?"

Buchanan said, "I don't know, but I got a notion."

"We had the hosses ready for 'em. Farnum wanted to give up, I know he did."

"Uh-huh. I expect he had a notion, too." Buchanan went back into the bank.

The people were in a circle now, holding to one another, still in shock. Farnum lay in his own blood.

Yeager said, "Conrad did it. I thought we were all goners. Farnum tried to stop him."

"Take your people out where you can breathe," Buchanan said. "Leave this to me."

He went to Farnum. The wound was in the chest. He examined it as best he could and called, "Bring a doctor, quick."

Farnum looked at him. He seemed suddenly very weary. He said, "Doctor won't do any good."

"You're a hell of a man," Buchanan

murmured. "You didn't want to hurt people who didn't get in your way."

"The gal—Cole wanted the gal. Drove him crazy. I saw it comin'. I saw it long ago—"

"Best not to talk," said Buchanan.

Blood ran from the corner of Farnum's mouth. "What's the difference? It was hell in that hole, Buchanan. Where I'm goin' it can't be any worse—gave you a good run, didn't I?"

"The best," said Buchanan. "You were tough."

"Glad . . . I didn't . . . kill you. Cassidy and them—did they track me?" His voice grew weaker with each word.

"No. They thought they got lucky."

"You . . . you took care of them?"

"Funny thing. Conrad threw me the means to wipe 'em out. A bad bunch, Farnum."

"I. . . shouldn't have killed Amsy Burke. Only thing I'm . . . sorry about."

"He made his play."

"He shouldn't have . . . And I shouldn't

have . . . Hell, there's a whole damn lot I shouldn't've done."

"It's done and done," said Buchanan.

Farnum coughed, bringing up more bright blood. "Cole?"

"He'll go back to Yuma, most likely. For life."

Farnum said, "He won't last. Not tough enough . . ."

"Uh-huh."

"The smart one. Always the smart one . . ."

"You were plenty smart stashing the loot here in a bank. Never heard of that one before."

"Cole . . . thought . . . he was . . . smarter." The voice was growing faint. The man had been right. There was no hope for him. Buchanan knelt beside him with mixed emotions.

"Smart don't always make a man," was all he could think of to say.

Farnum tried to breathe, failed. Buchanan bent close to hear him. "The rewards . . . you won't take 'em . . . one thing."

"I'm no bounty-hunter is right."

"Enough . . . to bury me . . . decent . . . would you?"

Buchanan said, "I'll see to that."

Farnum smiled. "Thanks, Buchanan . . . thanks."

He died. Buchanan stayed a long minute, looking at him, thinking about him. He had seen too many good men go wrong and die in this fashion. It was the way of the frontier, he supposed. No place for some people, the greatest of all for others. He arose stiffly, his shoulder aching from the bullet put into it by the dead man, feeling no rancor, only a deep sorrow.

He went outside. Conrad lay upon the walk. A doctor came bustling with his little black bag. Buchanan said, "No use to go in there. Get your undertaker. I'm payin' for the funeral."

Marshal Martin said, "This one had two guns hid away and a couple of knives. And four decks of cards."

"The cards are marked, you can bet on

that," Buchanan told him. "Fix him up, Doc. He's takin' a long ride."

"You don't want me to keep him here?"

"I doubt you could manage," Buchanan said. "You didn't find any keys?"

"Nope. Just a tiny file, sort of."

"Uh-huh," said Buchanan. "Look again. Then we'll take him back. Coco and me. We won't sleep much but we'll get him there."

He looked for Coco. Mary Jane was leaning upon him, her face streaked with soot and tears. Her eyes were bright, however.

She said, "I knew you were there, but I didn't see how you could help us."

Buchanan nodded toward the recumbent Conrad. "The Lord works somethin'-somethin' in his miraculous way, or words like that which I never get straight. He threw the dynamite to me is all."

Coco said, "I thought you was never gonna throw it back."

"The loot. They all wanted the loot. It's like a gold rush. Men go off their minds."

"Conrad wanted me," said the girl.

"So that helped drive him crazy," Buchanan said.

"They could have got out the back way, the two of them. He wouldn't go without me and the money from the safe."

"Uh-huh," said Buchanan. "They had high hopes, those two. They thought they could get to a railway before we caught up with 'em."

Coco said, "A smart pair. But they shouldn't have killed Amsy Burke."

"Uh-huh," said Buchanan. His shoulder hurt and he was suddenly very tired. "We better get us some grub. Then some rest. Then we got a long ride."

"Back to Yuma?"

"Back to Yuma with Conrad."

Mary Jane sighed, "All this way, all this trouble. And I get to go back to Yuma."

Buchanan regarded her. He smiled for the first time in a long while. "Why, Mary Jane, after Yuma, me and Coco are goin' up to the high country. We got friends up there. If you want to go along?"

"I don't have any money."

Buchanan said, "I never accept reward

money. In this case I'll make an exception. If you want to get outa Yuma."

She looked into his eyes. "I thought of you every day and night when they had me. You can believe it, now that you got me free . . . I'll go anywhere with you."

It sounded good. She was a sweet, lovely girl. The strain vanished. Even his pain lessened. He said, "Uh-huh. Then we'll do just that."

"Fishin' and huntin'," said Coco. "I fish. He hunts."

"He don't have to hunt for me," said Mary Jane. "I'll be right there."

Buchanan turned to speak with Yeager and the others. He accepted their gratitude, he was polite. He was also hungry. It came down to that, he needed food and sleep. It had not been an easy adventure. But he had known that from the start.